I AM THE FIRE OF TIME

JANE B. KATZ, a former English teacher and writer of curriculum materials, has a keen interest in establishing a secure place for ethnic literature in the school curriculum. In 1971 she wrote a radio series for young people on the lives of historical and contemporary Indian leaders. A continuing fascination with American Indian oral and written history led to the publication of two books for secondary school students in 1975: *We Rode the Wind: Recollections of 19th Century Plains Tribal Life* and *Let Me Be a Free Man: A Documentary History of Indian Resistance* that traces protest movements from 1607 to 1974 in the words of the Indians themselves. A former New Yorker, she lives in Minneapolis with her husband and two children.

I AM THE FIRE OF TIME

The Voices of Native American Women

edited by
JANE B. KATZ

A Dutton Paperback

NEW YORK E. P. DUTTON

Library of Congress Catalog Card Number 77-79801
ISBN: 0-525-47475-7
Published simultaneously in Canada by Clarke, Irwin & Company Limited, Toronto and Vancouver
10 9 8 7 6 5 4 3 2 1
First Edition

Photograph credits: Pomo girl (p. 1), Hopi mother and child (p. 8), reprinted from *The North American Indian* (New York: Johnson Reprint Corp., 1970), Supplement, vol. 3, pls. 486, 403./ Qahátika girl (p. 18), reprinted from *The North American Indian,* Supplement, vol. 1, pl. 56./ Delfina Cuero (p. 41), reprinted from *Autobiography of Delfina Cuero* (Los Angeles: Dawson's Book Shop, 1968), by permission of Mrs. Florence Shipek./ Mountain Wolf Woman (p. 56), reprinted from Nancy Oestreich Lurie, *Mountain Wolf Woman* (Ann Arbor: University of Michigan Press, 1961), by permission of University of Michigan Press./ Baffin Island Eskimo woman (p. 61), reprinted by permission of the Minister of Supply and Services, Ottawa./ On the beach—Chinook (p. 67), Embarking—Kutenai (p. 195), reprinted from *The North American Indian,* Supplement, vol. 2, pls. 292, 250./ Indian girl (p. 73), reprinted from Edgar S. Cahn, ed., *Our Brother's Keeper* (New York: New American Library, 1975), p. 24, by permission of New American Library./ Sioux woman (p. 92), reprinted from *Photographs and Poems by Sioux Children,* by permission of The Tipi Shop, Inc., sponsored by Indian Arts and Crafts Board, U.S. Department of Interior./ *In the Night Sky* (p. 98), *Young Woman* (p. 121), Drawing of an Eskimo woman (p. 167), *The Enchanted Owl* (p. 176), reprinted from W. T. Larmour, *The Art of the Canadian Eskimo,* issued by the Minister of Indian Affairs and Northern Development, copyright © 1968, by permission./ Ojibwe woman and child (p. 113), reprinted from Charles Brill, *Indian and Free* (Minneapolis: University of Minnesota Press, 1974), copyright © 1971 by Charles Brill, by permission./ Grace Black Elk (p. 134), reprinted from *Voices from Wounded Knee 1973* (Rooseveltown, N.Y.: Akwesasne Notes, 1974), by permission of *Akwesasne Notes.*/ Leslie Silko (p. 157), reprinted from Kenneth Rosen, ed., *The Man to Send Rain Clouds* (New York: The Viking Press, 1974), copyright © 1969 by Leslie Chapman, by permission of The Viking Press./ Buffy Sainte-Marie (p. 172), reprinted by permission of Vanguard Recording Society, New York./ Eskimo mother and child (p. 192), reprinted from *Dorset 75,* copyright © 1975 by M. F. Feheley Publishers Ltd., Toronto.

To my grandmother, Sophie Ruskay

UNTITLED

i am the fire of time.
the endless pillar
that has withstood death.
the support of an invincible nation.
i am the stars that have guided
lost men.
i am the mother of ten thousand
dying children.
i am the fire of time.
i am an indian woman!

Niki Paulzine

CONTENTS

Introduction xv

Part I From the Tribal World 1

1. A-a-aha, My Little One 7
2. And So I Grew Up 17
3. I Was Wed 32
4. Marriage Is a Sweet Thing When People Love Each Other 39
5. The Great Sea Sets Me Adrift 49
6. The Dead Dance with the Living 58
7. No One Cares for Our Corn Songs Now 65

Part II Voices of Today 73

1. I Keep Wondering How I Will Survive in This Strange Environment 80
2. Return to the Home We Made 91
3. I Wish I Could Learn to Talk Indian 109
4. A Legacy of Strength 120
5. Where Do We Find Justice in America? 129
6. To Walk in Beauty 152
7. In a Gentle Whirlwind I Was Shaken, Made to See on Earth in Many Ways 167

Sources and Credits 195

ILLUSTRATIONS

Pomo girl 1
Hopi mother and child 8
Sarah Winnemucca Hopkins 12
Qahátïka girl 18
Seminole girl 33
Delfina Cuero 41
Mountain Wolf Woman 56
Baffin Island Eskimo woman 61
On the beach—Chinook 67
Indian girl 73
Laura Wittstock 82
Sioux woman 92
In the Night Sky 98
Ojibwe woman and child 113
Young Woman 121
Constance Pinkerman, M.D. 124
Grace Black Elk 134
Gladys Bissonette 140
Ada Deer 150
Leslie Silko 157
Drawing of Eskimo woman 166
Buffy Sainte-Marie 171
The Enchanted Owl 175
Eskimo mother and child 191
Embarking—Kutenai 194

I am indebted to Professor Bea Medicine who was kind enough to critique the manuscript before it went to press. Her observations were invaluable.

I am grateful to Dr. Joseph Cash, director of the Institute of American Indian Studies at the University of South Dakota, Vermillion, for making transcripts of tapes from the Oral History Center available to me.

Rebecca Murray, Rosemary Christiansen, Loretta Ellis-Metoxen, Professors Chris Cavender, Frank Miller, and Roxanne Gudemann all provided insights, encouragement, and support.

I wish to thank my father, Harvey J. Bresler, a man of letters, for his astute and painstaking editing of the first draft; and Jack, Marc, and Mari for their patience.

Finally, I am indebted to *Akwesasne Notes* for fine, in depth coverage of Indian affairs; and to the many Native American women whose candor and grace made this book possible.

INTRODUCTION

"In the beginning was the word," writes Tsewaa, poet of the Tewa Nation. For the Native American living on tribal land, song was a means of communing with the forces of nature. Because everything in the universe had a spirit or a language of its own, men and women offered supplications to the sun, the moon, a rock, a tree, a bird; they called on unseen forces to assist with the processes of birth, germination, and healing. Repetition of a sacred formula, they felt, could bring a desired consequence. The Navajos sang to the corn:

> The waters of the dark clouds drop, drop,
> The rain descends.
> The waters from the corn leaves drop, drop . . .
> The corn grows up.[1]

The word served to link the individual to the creative life force present throughout the universe.

Song was also a bond between people. An individual communicated a vision or other personal experience in song. People sang of work, love, and death, of their hopes and fears, and of the tribal past. Song was a part of everyday conversation. Prose and poetry merged as the tale-spinners burst spontaneously into song.

In tribal culture, anyone could make songs, women as well as men. Although in some societies women sang primarily to win power or protection for their men, song-making was also a way for a woman to achieve status in the tribe. A sort of unofficial

[1] Translation by Washington Matthews, quoted in Margot Astrov, *American Indian Prose and Poetry* (New York: Capricorn Books, 1946), p. 13.

copyright system prevailed in many areas, making the song the property of the person who composed and sang it.

Part 1 of this collection focuses on the life cycle of North American tribes in song, prayer, and narrative. But these are not necessarily the most representative works of any particular tribe. Privacy is a part of the Indian tradition. Many native people will not expose their personal lives to scrutiny by outsiders. Some of their most sacred rites, for example, have been kept secret. Here then are fragments of a people's experience, a kaleidoscope of their customs and mores.

Native American poetry operates on many different levels and is thus difficult to translate literally. Code language masks the real significance of some of the holiest rituals. Symbols are profuse; a word that is understood on only a literal level by the uninitiated may suggest a whole constellation of experiences to the tribal member. Then too, figurative language is used extensively. In a Papago song recorded by Ruth Underhill: "Blue evening falls . . ./It sets the corn tassels trembling." In a Tewa poem, "The rain-showers hang from the sky." Compounding the problem for the translator, there are allusions to ancient myths and episodes in tribal history known only to insiders. The best translators—Frances Densmore, Ruth Bunzel, and others—lived with the tribes they studied and came to know the people intimately. Because they were poets as well as scholars, sensitive to the subtle nuances of language, their translations are as faithful as possible to the wording and spirit of the originals.

A number of oral histories from the tribal world are included in this book. Many of these, but by no means all, are translations. Some are the recollections shared by a few with anthropologists who lived in native communities and won the confidence of the people. These autobiographical narratives depict everyday life in graphic terms. In the *Autobiography of a Papago Woman* Maria Chona says: "As the mountain turns, it draws the clouds and the birds until they all float around it. . . ." She combines poetic gifts with a pragmatic view of life. She lets us inside her heart and mind.

Oral histories are reservoirs of a people's heritage and mythic knowledge. In her narrative, Maria Chona refers to a four-line song that tells the story of creation: "The song is short, because we understand so much." Maria Chona is a mystic; she transmits and thus preserves the wisdom of her ancestors. She is a tribal historian as well as a poet.

Indian oral literature—the poetry as well as the prose—belies the popular view of the native woman as a beast of burden. In fact, women fulfilled a multitude of functions essential to the life of the tribe, for instance in agriculture and the education of the children. For the most part, roles were assigned equitably. Men were frequently absent, in battle or hunting, so they relied on women to maintain stability in community life. And most women accepted this. In the total culture, there was a blending of male and female roles; harmony was the objective. A Navajo myth describes the contentment of early men and women, each of whom performed their assigned tasks. Then there was dissent; the men crossed the River of Separation. Soon, unable to live without their women they returned. From then on, men and women crossed the river together. Neither could get along without the other.

This is not to say, however, that all Native American women passively accepted the roles assigned to them. There is, in the oral literature, a tradition of independence, even of dissent. Maria Chona did not hesitate to leave a disloyal husband. In a Cheyenne legend, Corn Woman left an abusive husband. Ordered by her brother to return she did so but told her husband: "Don't ever try to beat me again. If you do, I'll fight you with whatever is at hand. I don't care if you kill me." From that day on he was her slave.[2] The Indian woman was neither subservient to her husband nor totally bound by custom.

Most Indian societies acknowledged woman's vital role in the creative process. In tribal ceremonies and lore she was portrayed as the giver of life. Pueblo peoples prayed for "female rain." Some tribes believed that woman had mystical power over the life cycle. Then, as now, the Indian woman was a cohesive force.

The nineteenth-century wars and upheavals left Native Ameri-

[2] E. Adamson Hoebel, *The Cheyennes* (New York: Holt, Rinehart & Winston, 1960), p. 26.

can society in disarray. Tribes were decimated and families scattered. But memories of the old life, the songs, and the chronicles survived. Through the oral literature the old passed on to the young their fading traditions and their indomitable will. Anthropologist Nancy Lurie reports that in the transition from a tribal existence to reservation life, native women suffered less dislocation than men, who lost their livelihood as hunters and warriors as well as their self-esteem. For wives and mothers, there was still a continuity of function, and as the men gradually found work away from the reservation, women assumed more and more responsibility at home. Some women also became breadwinners, working in offices and industry. Then they put their newly acquired skills to work revitalizing their communities.[3]

When tribalism regained strength in the mid-twentieth-century, women's voices were heard with increasing frequency. Ada Deer fought for political and economic survival of the Menominee tribe; Annie Dodge Wauneka championed the cause of the Navajo. On the national level LaDonna Harris, a Comanche, founded Americans for Indian Opportunity to attain jobs and education for all native peoples. Other women exerted leadership in the Indian way through the power of the word. Women poets and prose writers, emerging in the 1960s and 1970s, drew inspiration from the literature and lore of the tribal world. But they had to come to terms with the white man's desecration of their land and culture; with "graves among aloes and iris/graves among willows. . . ."[4] Their world had been shattered, and there was little of value left to them. Poverty and hopelessness were still facts of Indian life: "In the city of Gallup on the eastern edge of the Navajo Reservation there are drunks on the street before ten o'clock in the morning, and the rate of venereal infection is ten times the national average."[5] Nature was something to

[3] Nancy Oestreich Lurie, "A Legacy of Freedom," from *Look to the Mountain Top,* ed. Robert Iacopi (San Jose, Calif.: Gousha Publications, 1972), p. 33.

[4] Besmilr Brigham in "Mountains," from *Heaved from the Earth* (New York: Alfred A. Knopf, 1971).

[5] Earl Shorris, *Death of the Great Spirit* (New York: Simon & Schuster, 1971), p. 46.

cling to, something eternal. By reaffirming a bond with the universe, the Native American found that life had meaning.

Out of the traditions of the past but using the idiom of today, the contemporary Indian writer has forged a new style. It is candid and free, yet controlled. Animated by the rhythm and imagery of nature, it sings. Born in anger, softened by time, the prose and poetry of today express individuality, humanity, and pride. There is still a belief in the regenerative power of nature: "I arose from black fire," writes the poet Gladys Cardiff; and in the immortality of the word:

> I sing a little song,
> someone else's worn little song,
> but I sing it as if it were my own,
> my own dear little song.
>
> In this way, I play
> with a secondhand song,
> and give it life again.[6]

This collection is a tribute to the Native American literary tradition, the old with the new; and to the Native American woman, who, like the corn songs of the Pueblos, endures.

Minneapolis JANE KATZ

[6] *Eskimo Poetry from Canada and Greenland,* trans. Tom Lowenstein (Pittsburgh, Pa.: University of Pittsburgh Press, 1973), p. 54.

PART I
FROM THE TRIBAL WORLD

Pomo girl. Edward S. Curtis, 1924.

The world is full of songs

A vast number of tribal groups existed in North America before the coming of the white man. Each of these was a sovereign state with its own distinct language and government. Cultural patterns varied widely from tribe to tribe.

Each Indian nation had laws establishing lines of authority in peace and war, and in intertribal relations. Laws regulated crime and punishment. Some societies were matriarchal and matrilineal. Article 44 of the Iroquois Great Law of Peace reads:

> The lineal descent of the people of the Five Nations shall run in the female line. Women shall be considered the progenitors of the nation. They shall own the land and the soil. Men and women shall follow the status of their mothers.

Iroquois women determined who sat in the tribal councils and chose the war chiefs, thus wielding considerable political power.

Long before white Americans conceived of such "innovations" as welfare and a guaranteed income, North American Indian tribes demonstrated their concern for social justice. Those who adhered to ancient tribal ethics often shared food and possessions. Among the Kwakiutl, for example, a chief could gain distinction by giving away all his material wealth. A young Oglala chief was instructed to look after the poor, especially widows and orphans. In the extended families of Indian communities, the aged and infirm were provided for. Everyone, from the very young to the very old, had a useful task to perform. The individual was expected to contribute to the well-being of the group.

Through a carefully structured educational system, the old passed on the tribe's customs and values to the young, thus ensuring their preservation. Typically, children were reared in an atmosphere of relative freedom with few physical restraints. As they neared puberty they assumed more and more adult responsibilities. The good opinion of the group was a potent motivating force, and thus an effective instrument of social control.

Each tribal community had time-honored moral codes that set the pattern for male-female relationships. Those applying to a young woman at puberty, often based on taboo and the fear of primal forces, might circumscribe a girl's freedom of action.

They were designed to preserve the purity of young women, and the sanctity of the marriage institution. A woman might find her options in marriage restricted to a man chosen for her by her father or brother, often on the basis of material considerations. But she was not locked into an unhappy marriage for life. Divorce was fairly common; a Cheyenne woman, for example, could simply move back to her parents' tipi.

Although her husband often paid a bride price for her, a wife was by no means chattel: "In most . . . highly organized tribes, the woman was the sole master of her own body. Her husband or lover, as the case may be, acquired marital control over her person by her own consent."[1] Marriage was generally a close, working partnership; most marriages were monogamous. Cruelty to women was not condoned by public opinion. For the most part, when men and women acted out the roles their society prescribed for them, there was mutual respect. A wife's status depended on the cultural milieu of her tribe. Nineteenth-century records depicting Indian women as inferior to the men were written by men. And in answer to men, Sioux anthropologist Dr. Bea Medicine writes: "Of course, we did walk ten paces behind—that's documented—and the reason we did it, was to tell you where to go."[2]

The Indian nations possessed a spiritual philosophy based on centuries of accumulated wisdom and faith. The land they viewed as a sacred inheritance from the Great Spirit whom they worshiped in all of creation. Many Southwest tribes were unique in that they were able to remain on ancestral lands close to their roots and traditions; ancient, secret rituals expressing reverence for the sun, the rain, and the corn are still performed, and weld the people together. There were local religious movements, such as the Grand Medicine Rites of the Chippewa/Ojibwe,[3] but when the tribes were scattered, many such movements lost their hold over the people. Conversely, some religions gained momentum

[1] J. N. B. Hewitt, *Bureau of American Ethnology Bulletin,* no. 30.

[2] Bea Medicine, "Role and Function of Indian Women," *Indian Education,* National Indian Education Association (January 1977), p. 4.

[3] The spelling preferred by the Department of American Indian Studies, University of Minnesota, Minneapolis.

as dispersed tribes came into contact with each other. The Ghost Dance Cult of the Plains achieved, for a time, a pan-Indian impact. Its rituals were intended to bring about the return of dead Indian leaders and the wild game, and the disappearance of the white man; it served as an escape for Indians incarcerated in detention camps called "reservations" in the late nineteenth century. The Peyote Cult, known today as the Native American Church, synthesized elements of various tribal religions with Christian ritual, thus attracting Indians from many tribes and winning a firm foothold both on the reservations and in the cities.

In the late nineteenth century, most of the remaining tribal lands were divided into small plots. Indians accustomed to a semi-migrant existence were expected to settle down and become farmers. In some tribes planting had been women's work; men who might take up the hoe would expose themselves to ridicule. Much of the land was unsuitable for cultivation, and people who had worked the land communally were not trained to succeed as independent farmers. Facing starvation, many Indians sold out to whites.

Adaptation to white man's ways often meant survival. The autobiography of Waheenee,[4] a Hidatsa woman, records the process of acculturation that occurred within a generation. She grew up in an earth lodge that "belonged to the women who built it." Her son was educated in the white man's school and owned a farm and cattle. He taught his people "to follow the white man's road." In the early twentieth century, land seizures by government and industry and massive relocation programs accelerated the separation of the people from their land and their traditional ways. Modern technology altered economic life; native skills and crafts were often forgotten. The missionary and the public health nurse largely supplanted the shaman. Sanapia, a Comanche medicine woman skilled in the healing arts, saw herself as an anachronism: "My way is getting no good up to today. . . .

[4] *Waheenee: An Indian Girl's Story,* as told to Gilbert Wilson (Minneapolis, Minn.: Webb Publishing Company, 1921), p. 175.

Even my kids growing up like white people; and they think I'm just a funny old woman."[5]

Still, with women often leading the way, Native Americans made the transition from old roles to new life-styles. And they were not vanquished. In the words of a Cheyenne proverb: "A nation is not conquered until the hearts of its women are on the ground. Then it is done, no matter how brave its warriors or how strong its weapons."[6]

[5] *Sanapia; Comanche Medicine Woman,* ed. David E. Jones (New York: Holt, Rinehart & Winston, 1972), p. 31.

[6] Quoted by Shirley Hill Witt in "The Brave-Hearted Woman," *Akwesasne Notes* (Early Summer 1976), p. 17.

1.

A-A-AHA, MY LITTLE ONE

GRANDMOTHER'S PRAYER WHILE PRESENTING AN INFANT TO THE SUN ZUÑI

A newborn Zuñi infant was taken from its bed of sand and ritually presented to the sun. Mathilde Stevenson writes of this ceremony in her Religious Life of the Zuñi Child: *". . . The first object the child is made to behold at the very dawn of its existence is the sun, the great object of their worship"; then the grandmother recited this prayer.*

. . . May your road be fulfilled.
Reaching to the road of your sun father,
When your road is fulfilled.
In your thoughts may we live,
May we be the ones whom your thoughts will embrace.
For this, on this day
To our sun father,
We offer prayer meal.
To this end:
May you help us all to finish our roads.

Hopi mother and child. Edward S. Curtis, 1924.

FOR ME AND MY FIRST CHILD TO LIVE
DELFINA CUERO DIEGUEÑO

The Kumeyaay (Diegueño) Indians, a semisedentary people, occupied villages scattered over southern San Diego County, California. Although some inland villages became reservations, by the early twentieth century the expanding non-Indian population forced the coastal villagers to move. So began a trek to Diegueño territory in Baja California where they live today. During the upheaval, most of their traditional culture became extinct. With the aid of an interpreter, an elderly refugee told what she remembered of the old life to Florence Shipek who published the Autobiography of Delfina Cuero. *Ms. Cuero was explicit about birth and the care of the young child.*

I had my babies by myself. I didn't have any help from anybody . . . I did what I had been taught. I used xaʔ a·nayul (mint family) or kʷa·s (sumac) to bathe in and I drank a little kʷa·s tea also.

I dug a little place and built a hot fire and got hot ashes. I put something, bark or cloth, over the ashes and put the baby in it to keep the baby warm. . . .

To keep the navel from getting infected, I burned cowhide, or any kind of skin, till crisp, then ground it. I put this powder on the navel. I did this and no infection started in my babies . . . When each baby was new born, I bathed it in elderberry blossom or willow bark tea. . . . The afterbirth is buried in the floor of the house.

I did all this myself. When my children were older, if they got sick, I used herbs. That is all I used and my children got well again. There are herbs for stomach pains, colds, toothaches, and everything that the Indians knew. There is a real good one to stop bleeding right away from a bad cut. There is another good one for bad burns and to stop infection . . . there is another herb . . . that the Indians used to use to keep from having babies every year. They are hard to find now because we can't go everywhere to look for them anymore.

I named all of my children myself. I didn't know anything about baptizing them then; I just went ahead like the Indians did and gave them names. When my oldest child was a year or two old, they had a party to welcome him to the group. Everybody got together and they built a big ramada for me and they brought their food together. We had a big fire. I had an uncle that led the singing and dancing. He led a big fire dance. They circled around the fire hand in hand, and following each other, and jumping with both feet and singing. . . . All the people brought presents for the baby—baskets, ollas,[1] food, mud dolls, or bow and arrows, whatever was right to start the child . . .

The fire dance was religious; they danced all night till the sun came up. The songs that go with it have to be sung in the right order, from early evening until dawn. There is a song for each time of the night and as the sun is rising . . . That is what they did for me and my first child to live. They might have done more before, but they don't even do this now.

[1] *Olla:* earthen pot or jar used for holding water or for cooking.

LULLABY TEWA

In the south the cloud flower blossoms,
And now the lightning flashes,
And now the thunder clashes,
And now the rain comes down;
A-a-aha, a-a-aha, my little one.

THE FATHER ASSUMES ALL HIS WIFE'S WORK
SARAH WINNEMUCCA HOPKINS PAIUTE

Sarah Winnemucca Hopkins was born in 1844 on tribal lands in Nevada. She was educated in mission schools where she became fluent in the English language. In 1883 she published her autobiography, Life Among the Piutes,[2] *an account of her people's traditional ways. She described ceremonies following the birth of a first child.*

Both father and mother fast from all flesh, and the father goes through the labor of piling the wood for twenty-five days, and assumes all his wife's household work during that time. If he does not do his part in the care of the child, he is considered an outcast. Every five days his child's basket is changed for a new one, and . . . put up into a tree, and the child put into a new and ornamented basket.

All this respect shown to the mother and child makes the parents feel their responsibility, and makes the tie between parents and children very strong. The young mothers often get together and exchange their experiences about the attentions of their husbands; and inquire of each other if the fathers did their duty to their children, and were careful of their wives' health . . .

The poor people have the same ceremonies, but do not make a feast of it, for want of means.

[2] The spelling used in the original edition.

Sarah Winnemucca Hopkins. Courtesy Nevada State Museum, Carson City.

THERE WAS LOVE IN MY HOME
HELEN SEKAQUAPTEWA HOPI

Sekaquaptewa was born in 1898 in Old Oraibi, one of eleven Hopi villages in southeastern Arizona. In this arid, plateau country surrounded by rocky cliffs, her people had lived in relative stability since the time of Columbus; their ancient life-style was affected little by changes in the outside world. Sekaquaptewa recorded childhood experiences in her autobiography, Me and Mine: The Life Story of Helen Sekaquaptewa, *as told to Louise Udall.*

When I was twenty days old I was taken by my mother and my paternal grandmother to the eastern edge of the mesa.[3] There, in accord with Hopi custom, as the sun came up, they petitioned to him to take notice of this little Hopi girl baby and bless her with life, health, and a family. . . .

The house where I was born stood for years on the northwest edge of Old Oraibi mesa. The house was torn down and the timbers reused in other houses, but the earliest memories of my life there still live in my heart. There was love in my home, and I felt happy and secure during my childhood. I began learning about life just like all children do, from imitating my elders. My mother seemed to be grinding corn most of the time . . .

I spent many happy hours playing pleasant games with other children in the village plaza. Sometimes we even ventured out among the rocks and cedar trees in games of chase and hide-and-seek.

[3] *Mesa:* a flat area bounded by steep rock walls.

MY PEOPLE TEACH THEIR CHILDREN
SARAH WINNEMUCCA HOPKINS PAIUTE

Paiute communities educated their children according to a pragmatic, "learn by doing" philosophy. The tribal group was interdependent; people had to work together harmoniously. Thus, human relations skills were taught at an early age, as shown in this excerpt from Life Among the Piutes.

Our children are very carefully taught to be good . . . My people teach their children never to make fun of anyone, no matter how they look. If you see your brother or sister doing something wrong, look away, or go away from them. If you make fun of bad persons, you make yourself beneath them.

Be kind to all, both poor and rich, and feed all that come to your wigwam, and your name can be spoken of by everyone far and near. In this way you will make many friends for yourself. Be kind to bad and good, for you don't know your own heart.

This is the way my people teach their children. It was handed down from father to son for many generations. I never in my life saw our children rude as I have seen white children and grown people in the streets.

WOMAN'S SONG FROM *THE HAKO* PAWNEE

Alice Fletcher translated The Hako, *an intricate ritual-drama of the Pawnee. In solemn rites that extended over many days, these people expressed their dependence on the supernatural for the gifts of life, and on the family for security. They conveyed, too, a sense of oneness with the human family. Children were anointed; in them was the promise of continuity of the tribe and of life.*

I know not if the voice of man can reach to the sky;
I know not if the mighty one will hear as I pray;
I know not if the gifts I ask will all granted be;
I know not if the word of old we truly can hear;
I know not what will come to pass in our future days;
I hope that only good will come, my children, to you.

I HAD A HAPPY CHILDHOOD
PITSEOLAK ASHOONA CAPE DORSET ESKIMO

Pitseolak Ashoona, the Eskimo graphic artist, was born in a skin tent around the turn of the century on Nottingham Island in Canada's Hudson Bay Area. Her autobiography Pitseolak: Pictures Out of My Life *was recorded in Eskimo by Dorothy Eber, then translated into English. Pitseolak told what it was like to be a child of migrants in the harsh arctic environment.*

My name is Pitseolak, the Eskimo word for the sea pigeon. When I see pitseolaks over the sea, I say, "There go those lovely birds—that's me flying! . . ."

The year I was born my parents and three brothers began a long trip. They . . . set out for Baffin Island to join relatives . . . The next spring they crossed the Hudson Strait and arrived . . . in the place where Cape Dorset is today . . . These were long journeys and dangerous too, when the waters were rough, but I didn't know—I was still being carried on the back of my mother.

We made all these travels in a sealskin boat. Such boats had wooden frames that were covered with skins. They used to be called the women's boats because they were sewn by the women. . . .

But even in my childhood these sealskin boats were already disappearing. My first memory of life is when we stopped in Lake Harbour, on our way back from Frobisher Bay to Cape Dorset, to buy a wooden boat . . . It was while my father bought the wooden boat that I first saw houses and that I saw the first white man. I was scared . . .

I had a happy childhood. I was always healthy and never sick. I had a large family—three brothers and a sister—and we were always happy to be together. We lived in the old Eskimo way. We would pick up and go to different camps—we were free to move anywhere . . . it depended on whether a person wanted to go far or be near a settlement. My father hunted in the old way—with a bow and arrow. He had a shotgun but he didn't use it. Sometimes there were bad winters, and we would go hungry but there was no starvation. . . .

2.

AND SO I GREW UP

CORN GRINDING SONG ZUÑI

A young girl of the pueblos was instructed at an early age in that most essential skill, the grinding of corn. She learned to kneel in the stone-grinding trough called metate *and to rub one stone over another, swaying and singing as she worked. Often other young women joined in, and the grinding became a joyous social event.*

Oh, my lovely mountain
Oh, my lovely mountain

High up in the sky
See Rainmakers[1] seated,
Hither come the rain clouds now,

Behold, yonder
All will soon be abloom
Where the flowers spring
Tall shall grow the youthful corn plants.

[1] *Rainmakers:* spirits of dead Zuñis who come from the world of the dead to make rain for the Zuñi people.

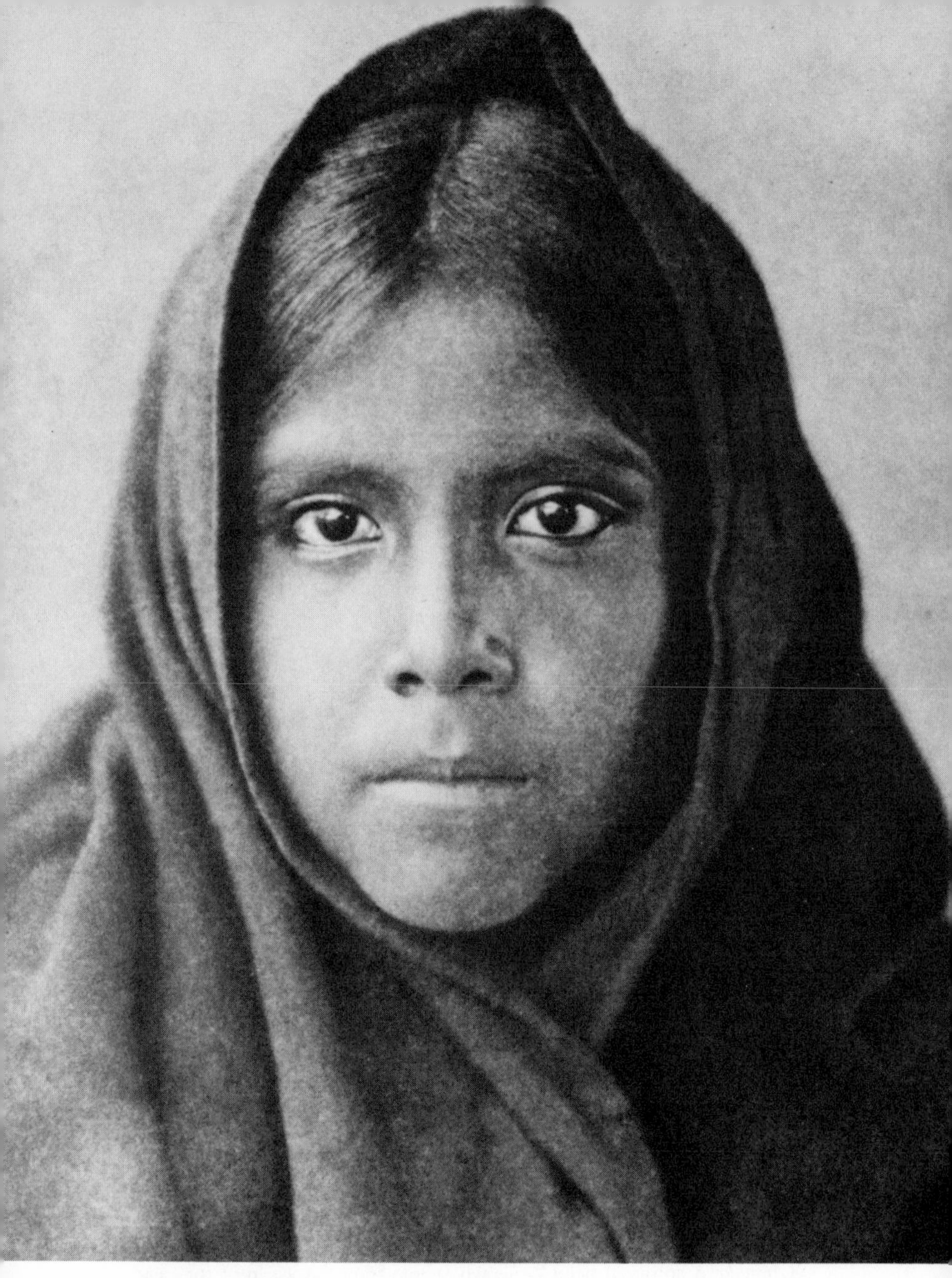

Qahátĭka girl. Edward S. Curtis, 1907.

THERE IS A WHITE SHELL MOUNTAIN IN THE OCEAN
MARIA CHONA PAPAGO

In 1936, anthropologist Ruth Underhill published her Autobiography of a Papago Woman, *a record of life in a tradition-bound Papago community in Arizona. Dr. Underhill wrote: "The Northern part of the reservation ferments liquor from the giant cactus fruit and drinks it ritually as a magic to saturate the earth with rain." Her ninety-year-old informant, Maria Chona, recalled her childhood.*

We lived at Mesquite Root and my father was chief there. That was a good place, high up among the hills, but flat, with a little wash where you could plant corn. Prickly pear grew there so thick that in summer, when you picked the fruit, it was only four steps from one bush to the next. And cholla cactus grew and there were ironwood trees. Good nuts they have! There were birds flying around, doves and woodpeckers, and a big rabbit sometimes in the early morning, and quails running across the flat land. Right above us was Quijotoa Mountain, the one where the cloud stands up high and white when we sing for rain.

We lived in a grass house, and our relatives, all around us on the smooth flat land, had houses that were the same. Round our houses were, with no smoke hole and just a little door where you crawled in on hands and knees. That was good. The smoke could go out anywhere through the thatch and the air could come in. All our family slept on cactus fiber mats against the wall, pushed tight against it so centipedes and scorpions could not crawl in. There was a mat for each two children, but no, nothing over us. When we were cold, we put wood on the fire.

Early in the morning, in the month of Pleasant Cold, when we had all slept in the house to keep warm, we would wake in the dark to hear my father speaking.

"Open your ears, for I am telling you a good thing. Wake up and listen. Open your ears. Let my words enter them." He spoke in a low voice, so quiet in the dark. Always our fathers spoke to us like that, so low that you thought you were dreaming.

"Wake up and listen. You boys, you should go out and run. So you will be swift in time of war. You girls, you should grind the corn. So you will feed the men and they will fight the enemy. You should practice running. So, in time of war, you may save your lives."

For a long time my father talked to us like that, for he began when it was black dark. I went to sleep, and then he pinched my ear. "Wake up! Do not be idle!"

Then we got up. It was the time we call morning-stands-up, when it is dark but there are white lines in the east. Those are the white hairs of Elder Brother who made us. He put them there so we can know when day is coming and we can go out to look for food. . . .

Then we made our toilet. We washed our faces in a little cold water, but we did not bathe. Rubbing yourself with earth does just as well. Then the older girls painted themselves with beautiful red paint, all in dots and splashes. I went out to play. . . .

Those girls had nothing on above the waist. We did not wear clothes then. They had strips of handwoven cloth in front and behind, tied around their waists with a string, for we did not know how to sew them together. The girls used to crawl laughing out of the houses, with their long black hair hanging to their waists, and they would pick up their carrying nets. Fine nets we used to have in those days, all dyed with red and blue. Shaped like a cone they were, with tall red sticks to keep them in shape. When the net was on a girl's back, those red sticks would stand up on either side of her face. We used to think a pretty young girl looked best that way. That was how the men liked to see her. . . .

I used to help my mother. When I was very little I began to grind the seeds, just for a short time. When I was ten years old I did it all, for then a daughter should be able to take over the work and let her mother sit down to baskets. But I am telling you about the early days when I could only grind a little. Then we pulled the grinding slab inside the house by the fire and my mother knelt behind it. I picked the dirt out of the seeds and handed them to her, and the pot boiled on the hearth on the three stones that we kept there. . . .

At last the giant cactus grew ripe on all the hills. It made us laugh to see the fruit on top of all the stalks, so many, and the men would point to it and say: "See the liquor growing." We went to pick it, to the same place where we always camped, and every day my mother and all the women went out with baskets. They knocked the fruit down with cactus poles. It fell on the ground and all the red pulp came out. Then I picked it up, and dug it out of the shell with my fingers, and put it in my mother's basket. She told me always to throw down the skins with the red inside uppermost, because that would bring the rain.

It was good at cactus camp. When my father lay down to sleep at night, he would sing songs about the cactus liquor. And we could hear songs in my uncle's camp across the hill. Everybody sang. We felt as if a beautiful thing was coming. Because the rain was coming and the dancing and the songs. . . .

Then the little rains began to come. We had jugs of the juice that my mother had boiled, and all the women carried them in their nets as we came running down the mountain back to our village. Much, much liquor we made, and we drank it to pull down the clouds, for that is what we call it. I was too little to drink. They put me on the housetop with my older sister. Our jars of liquor were up there, too. The housetop was the only safe place.

We heard the people singing over by the council house:

> There sits the magician of the east
> Holding the rain by the hand
> The wind holding by the hand
> He sits.

Then they began to drink. Making themselves beautifully

drunk, for that is how our words have it. People must all make themselves drunk like plants in the rain and they must sing for happiness. We heard them singing all day all over the village. Then my father and mother came and stood by the house where we were on the roof, with many relatives. Oh, they were very happy. "Reach us down a new jar from the roof," they said. So my sister handed it down. Then they gave it to drink to all the relatives whom they loved. And each, when he had drunk, sang a song.

The next day a relative came and said: "Your father and mother are out by the arroyo sleeping. Let a child go and stay with them until they wake." So my sister went. My brothers were drunk, too, but we did not know where. At last my father and mother awoke and came home very happy. For many days they sang. . . .

My father would lie quietly upon his mat with my mother beside him and the baby between them. At last he would start slowly to tell us about how the world began. This is a story that can be told only in winter when there are no snakes about, for if the snakes heard, they would crawl in and bite you. But in winter when snakes are asleep, we tell these things. Our story about the world is full of songs, and when the neighbors heard my father singing they would open our door and step in over the high threshold. Family by family they came, and we made a big fire and kept the door shut against the cold night. When my father finished a sentence, we would all say the last word after him. If anyone went to sleep, he would stop. He would not speak anymore. But we did not go to sleep.

My father's story told us all about why we hold our big feasts, because Elder Brother showed us how in the beginning of the world. My father went to those feasts and he took us, too, because my father was a song maker and he had visions even if he was not a medicine man. He always made a song for the big harvest festival, the one that keeps the world going right and that only comes every four years.

We all went then, from all over our country, to the Place of the Burnt Seeds. We camped together, many, many families together, and we made images of the beautiful things that make life good for the Desert People, like clouds and corn and squash and deer. The men sang about those things and my father made songs. When I was about eight years old, my father once made an image of a mountain out of cactus ribs covered with white cloth. He had dreamed about that mountain and this is the song he made:

> There is a white shell mountain[2] in the ocean
> Rising half out of the water.
> Green scum floats on the water
> And the mountain turns around.

The song is very short because we understand so much. We can understand how tall and white the mountain was, and that white shell is something precious, such as the handsome men of old used to have for their necklaces, and it would shine all across the earth as they walked. We understand that as that mountain turns, it draws the clouds and the birds until they all float around it. All those things my father told me when he used to sing that song in our house. I did not understand, though, when I was a little girl and went to the harvest festival. I was afraid of the singers with their masks. There were clowns with masks, too, white masks with little holes for eyes. The clowns bless people, and one put his hand out to bless me, but I ducked under it and ran.

Only afterward I used to dream of the white clown. Perhaps it was because someday I was going to marry one. It may be, for I have magic dreams. I am one who understands things.

[2] *White shell mountain:* in Papago mythology the abode of White Shell Woman who, like the Earth Mother, was believed to have created the world.

A HAPPY, CONTENTED INDIAN GIRL
WAHEENEE HIDATSA

Waheenee, also known as Buffalo-Bird Woman, was born in 1840 in an earth lodge in the picturesque Village of the Willows in North Dakota. There, alongside their allies the Mandans, the Hidatsa lived in harmony, farming and hunting just as their ancestors had done. In her native tongue, with her son Edward Goodbird as translator, Waheenee dictated her memoirs to Gilbert Wilson. Waheenee: An Indian Girl's Story *was published in 1921.*

My father's lodge, or, better, my mothers' lodge—for an earth lodge belonged to the women who built it—was more carefully constructed than most winter lodges were. Earth was heaped thick on the roof to keep in the warmth; and against the sloping walls without were leaned thorny rosebushes, to keep the dogs from climbing up and digging holes in the roof. The fireplace was a round, shallow pit, with edges plastered smooth with mud. Around the walls stood the family beds, six of them, covered each with an old tent skin on a frame of poles.

A winter lodge was never very warm; and, if there were old people or children in the family, a second, or "twin lodge," was often built. This was a small lodge with roof peaked like a tipi but covered with bark and earth. A covered passage led from it to the main lodge.

The twin lodge had two uses. In it the grandparents or other feeble or sickly members of the family could sit, snug and warm on the coldest day; and the children of the household used it as a playhouse.

I can just remember playing in our twin lodge, and making little feasts with bits of boiled tongue or dried berries that my mothers gave me. I did not often get to go out of doors; for I was not a strong little girl, and, as the winter was a hard one, my mothers were at pains to see that I was kept warm. I had a tiny robe, made of a buffalo-calf skin, that I drew over my little buckskin dress; and short girls' leggings over my ankles. In the twin lodge, as in the larger earth lodge, the smoke hole let in plenty of fresh air.

My mothers had a scant store of corn and beans, and some strings of dried squashes; and they had put by two or three sacks of dried prairie turnips. A mess of these turnips was boiled now and then and was very good. Once, I remember, we had a pudding: dried prairie turnips pounded to a meal and boiled with dried Juneberries. Such a pudding was sweet, and we children were fond of it.

To eke out our store of corn and keep the pot boiling my father hunted much of the time. . . .

And so I grew up, a happy, contented Indian girl, obedient to my mothers, but loving them dearly. I learned to cook, dress skins, embroider, sew with awl and sinew, and cut and make moccasins, clothing, and tent covers. There was always plenty of work to do, but I had time to rest, and to go to see my friends; and I was not given tasks beyond my strength. My father did the heavy lifting, if posts or beams were to be raised. "You are young, daughter," he would say. "Take care you do not overstrain!" He was a kind man, and helped my mothers and me whenever we had hard work to do.

For my industry in dressing skins, my clan aunt, Sage, gave me a woman's belt. It was as broad as my three fingers, and covered with blue beads. One end was made long, to hang down before me. Only a very industrious girl was given such a belt. She could not buy or make one. No relative could give her the belt; for a clan aunt, remember, was not a blood relative. To wear a woman's belt was an honor. . . .

In these years of my girlhood my mothers were watchful of all that I did. We had big dances in the village, when men and women sang, drums beat loud, and young men, painted and feathered, danced and yelled to show their brave deeds. I did not go to these dances often, and when I did my mothers went with me. Ours was one of the better families of the tribe, and my mothers were very careful of me.

. . . BEING A YOUNG WOMAN IS EVIL FOX

The Autobiography of a Fox Indian Woman *was published by Truman Michelson in 1918. In his introduction Michelson wrote: "It is not lawful for a Fox woman who is menstruating to eat with others; if . . . she touches a tree, the tree will die." An unidentified woman recalled her initiation into puberty; her mother gave detailed instructions.*

I was thirteen . . . and I was told: "Now is the time when you must watch yourself; at last you are nearly a young woman. Do not forget this which I tell you. You might ruin your brothers if you are not careful. The state of being a young woman is evil. The manitous[3] hate it. If anyone is blessed by a manitou, if he eats with a young woman he is then hated . . . At the time when . . . you become a young woman, you are to hide yourself . . ."

I went and laid down in the middle of the thick forest there. I was crying as I was frightened. It was almost the middle of summer after we had done our hoeing. After a while my mother got tired of waiting for me. She came to seek me . . .

"Come, stop crying. It's just the way with us women. We have been made to be that way. Nothing will happen to you . . . Now, today, as it is warm weather, you may swim slowly as you like . . . Lie covered up. Do not try to look around. I shall go and make a wickiup[4] for you," I was told . . .

I was shut off by twigs all around. There was brush piled up so that I could not see through it. There was only a little space, where I lived, to cook outside . . .

[3] *Manitou:* the Great Spirit of the Woodland tribes.

[4] *Wickiup:* a shelter consisting of a frame, somewhat conical-shaped, covered by reeds, grass, or brush.

And my grandmother[5] would keep on giving me instructions there, telling me how to lead a good life . . . "If you observe the way your mother makes anything, you would do well, my grandchild. . . . Today, to be sure, things are changing. When I was a young woman, I fasted eight days. We always fasted until we were grown up," my grandmother told me.

"Do not touch your hair; it might all come off. And do not eat sweet things. And if what tastes sour is eaten, one's teeth will come out . . . Now the men will think you are mature as you have become a young woman, and they will be desirous of courting you . . . If you are immoral your brothers will be ashamed, and your mother's brothers.[6]

WE WERE NEVER AT ODDS WITH ONE ANOTHER
MOUNTAIN WOLF WOMAN WINNEBAGO

Mountain Wolf Woman was born in Wisconsin in 1885, in a log cabin built by her father, a homesteader. At a time when most Indians were forced onto reservations, her family was permitted to remain on tribal land. In her autobiography, Mountain Wolf Woman: Sister of Crashing Thunder, *dictated to Nancy Oestreich Lurie, she told of a lifelong struggle to reconcile the old ways of her people with the new.*

We used coals from the fire to blacken our cheeks and we did not eat all day. I used to play outside but my older sister used to sit indoors and weave yarn belts. When father returned from hunting in the evening he used to say to us, "Go cry to the Thunders." When father was ready to eat he would give us tobacco and say to us, "Here, go cry to the Thunders." Just as it was getting dark my sister and I used to go off a certain distance and she would say

[5] *Grandmother* was an honorary term. In this case, another old woman of the tribe fulfilled this function.

[6] A girl's maternal uncle often served as her mentor.

to me, "Go stand by a tree and I am going to go farther on." We used to stand there and look at the stars and cry to the Thunders. This is what we used to sing: "Oh, Good Spirits/Will they pity me? Here am I, pleading."

We used to sing and scatter tobacco, standing there and watching the stars and the moon. We used to cry because, after all, we were hungry. We used to think we were pitied. We really wanted to mean what we were saying.

When we finished with our song, we scattered tobacco at the foot of the tree and returned home. . . .

We were never at odds with one another, nor quarreling nor scolding one another. Mother and father never scolded any of us; however, we were probably well behaved. They never used to scold me. Now children are not like that. They are even against their own parents. But my children were never against me. I have six daughters and two sons. My own children are big now. They would never say "shut up" to me, none of them were ever against me.

When I was a little girl I went to school when I was nine years old. They let me go to school. My oldest brother said I should go to school. He said he liked to hear women speak English. They let me attend school at Tomah [Wisconsin] and then I went to school at Wittenberg [Wisconsin]. Then I knew many things, but not much anymore. I did not even finish the sixth grade. It was in the spring before school was out that they made me stop attending school.[7] I went there when I was thirteen years old. There I became a Christian; Lutheran they called that kind of Christian. They baptized me and confirmed me and since then I am a Christian . . .

Mother told me how it is with little girls when they become women. "Sometime," she said, "that is going to happen to you. From about the age of thirteen years this happens to girls. When that happens to you, run to the woods and hide someplace. You should not look at anyone, not even a glance. If you look at a

[7] She was brought back home so that her brothers could find a husband for her.

man, you will contaminate his blood. Even a glance will cause you to be an evil person. When women are in that condition, they are unclean." Once, after our return to grandfather's house, I was in that condition when I awoke in the morning.

Because mother had told me to do so, I ran quite far into the woods where there were some bushes. The snow was still on the ground and the trees were just beginning to bud. In the woods there was a broken tree and I sat down under this fallen tree. I bowed my head with my blanket wrapped over me and there I was, crying and crying. Since they had forbidden me to look around, I sat there with my blanket over my head. I cried. Then, suddenly I heard the sound of voices. My sister Hińakega and my sister-in-law found me. Because I had not come back in the house, they had looked for me. They saw my tracks in the snow, and by my tracks they saw that I ran. They trailed me and found me. "Stay here," they said, "we will go and make a shelter for you," and they went home again. Near the water's edge of a big creek, at the rapids of East Fork River, they built a little wigwam. They covered it with canvas. They built a fire and put straw there for me, and then they came to get me. There I sat in the little wigwam. I was crying. It was far, about a quarter of a mile from home. I was crying and I was frightened. Four times they made me sleep there. I never ate. There they made me fast.[8] That is what they made me do. After the third time that I slept, I dreamed.

There was a big clearing. I came upon it, a big, wide open field, and I think there was a rise of land there. Somewhat below this rise was the big clearing. There, in the wide meadow, there were all kinds of horses, all colors. I must have been one who dreamed about horses. I believe that is why they always used to give me horses.

[8] Girls fasted in the hope that the spirits would reward them with a long and useful life, a good husband, and a large family of healthy children.

THE CHILDREN WOULD HAVE TO GO TO SCHOOL
HELEN SEKAQUAPTEWA HOPI

Laws making school attendance compulsory were a threat to Hopi parents, who were accustomed to instruct their children at home. They feared that outside intervention would undermine traditional ways. Some submitted to pressure; others remained hostile, and when school officials came with the truant officer to get the children, many were hidden. Sekaquaptewa recalls the time in 1906 when troops surrounded her village in Arizona, lined up all children of school age, put the protesting fathers under arrest, and took the children forcibly to school.

We were now loaded into wagons hired from and driven by our enemies . . . We were taken to the schoolhouse in New Oraibi, with military escort. We slept on the floor of the dining room that night. . . .

It was after dark when we reached the Keams Canyon boarding school and were unloaded and taken into the big dormitory, lighted with electricity. I had never seen so much light at night. I was all mixed up and thought it was daytime . . . There were not enough beds so they put mattresses on the floor . . .

Evenings we would gather in a corner and cry softly so the matron would not hear and scold or spank us. I would try to be a comforter, but in a little while I would be crying too. I can still hear the plaintive little voices saying, "I want to go home. I want my mother." We didn't understand a word of English and didn't know what to say or do . . .

I was really serious at school, even from the beginning, but some of the teachers were unkind to me. Once when I gave the wrong answer, the teacher boxed me real hard on the ear. I had earache after that, every night for a long time, and I can't hear very well out of that ear. . . .

The teachers and matrons gave us responsibility and depended upon us as we grew older. When I was fifteen, I was in charge of the post laundry during the summer. This served the teachers and other government employees. It was a big job and hard work doing up white shirts with pleated fronts and stiff starched collars, and equally starched white cotton dresses. The washing machines were big ones and were run by steam from the powerhouse. The irons were heated on a wood stove. I ran the machines and had experience in sorting and checking the bundles. I was paid $15 a month.

What I earned myself was the only money I ever had. We were so poor that my parents didn't send me any money. Sometimes I worked in the homes of government employees . . .

I enjoyed school and was eager to learn. I was a good reader and got good grades. The teachers favored me and whenever visitors came they always called on me to recite. I was not the most popular girl in school and my ability did not help me socially, it only made the others jealous. The girls would get me out in the yard and say, "You are quite an important person in the classroom, but out here you are nothing." I would answer, "Isn't that what we are here for, to learn?"

3.

I WAS WED

YOUNG WOMAN'S SONG OJIBWE (CHIPPEWA)

Oh
I am thinking
I have found
my lover.

AND SO I WAS WED
WAHEENEE HIDATSA

Waheenee was the daughter of Small Ankle, a capable and progressive chief of the Hidatsa. In her autobiography, Waheenee: An Indian Girl's Story, *she described her people's traditional courting and marriage procedures.*

I was eighteen years old the Bent-Enemy-Killed winter; for we Hidatsas reckoned by winters, naming each for something that happened in it. An old man named Hanging Stone then lived in the village. He had a stepson named Magpie, a handsome young man and a good hunter.

One morning Hanging Stone came into our lodge. It was a little while after our morning meal, and I was putting away the wooden bowls that we used for dishes. . . .

Seminole girl. Photograph courtesy Florida Department of Commerce, Tallahassee.

Hanging Stone walked up to my father and laid his right hand on my father's head. "I want you to believe what I say," he cried. "I want my boy to live in your good family. I am poor, you are rich; but I want you to favor us and do as I ask."

He went over to my mothers and did likewise, speaking the same words to both. He then strode out of the lodge.

Neither my father nor my mothers said anything, and I did not know at first what it all meant. My father sat for a while, looking at the fire. At last he spoke, "My daughter is too young to marry. When she is older I may be willing."

Toward evening Hanging Stone and his relatives brought four horses and three flintlock guns to our lodge. He tied the four horses to the drying stage outside. They had good bridles, with chains hanging to the bits. On the back of each horse was a blanket and some yards of calico, very expensive in those days.

Hanging Stone came into the lodge. "I have brought you four horses and three guns," he said to my father.

"I must refuse them," answered Small Ankle. "My daughter is too young to marry."

Hanging Stone went away, but he did not take his horses with him. My father sent them back by some young men.

The evening of the second day after, Hanging Stone came again to our lodge. As before, he brought the three guns and gifts of cloth, and four horses; but two of these were hunting horses. A hunting horse was one fleet enough to overtake a buffalo, a thing that few of our little Indian ponies could do. Such horses were costly and hard to get. A family that had good hunting horses had always plenty of meat.

After Hanging Stone left, my father said to his wives, "What do you think about it?"

"We would rather not say anything," they answered. "Do as you think best."

"I know this Magpie," said my father. "He is a kind young man. I have refused his gifts once, but I see his heart is set on having our daughter. I think I shall agree to it."

Turning to me he spoke: "My daughter, I have tried to raise

you right. I have hunted and worked hard to give you food to eat. Now I want you to take my advice. Take this man for your husband. Try always to love him. Do not think in your heart, 'I am a handsome young woman, but this man, my husband, is older and not handsome.' Never taunt your husband. Try not to do anything that will make him angry."

I did not answer yes or no to this; for I thought, "If my father wishes me to do this, why that is the best thing for me to do." I had been taught to be obedient to my father. I do not think white children are taught so, as we Indian children were taught.

For nigh a week my father and my two mothers were busy getting ready the feast foods for the wedding. On the morning of the sixth day, my father took from his bag a fine weasel-skin cap and an eagle-feather war bonnet. The first he put on my head; the second he handed to my sister, Cold Medicine. "Take these to Hanging Stone's lodge," he said. . . .

I lifted the skin door—it was an old-fashioned one swinging on thongs from the beam overhead—and entered the lodge. Hanging Stone sat on his couch against the puncheon fire screen. I went to him and put the weasel-skin cap on his head. The young man who was to be my husband was sitting on his couch, a frame of poles covered with a tent skin. Cold Medicine and I went over and shyly sat on the floor nearby.

The kettles of feast foods had been set down near the fireplace, and the three horses tied to the corn stage without. Hanging Stone had fetched my father four horses. We reckoned the weasel cap and the war bonnet as worth each a horse; and, with these and our three horses, my father felt he was going his friend one horse better. It was a point of honor in an Indian family for the bride's father to make a more valuable return gift than that brought him by the bridegroom and his friends.

As we two girls sat on the floor, with ankles to the right, as Indian women always sit, Magpie's mother filled a wooden bowl with dried buffalo meat pounded fine and mixed with marrow fat and set it for my sister and me to eat. We ate as much as we could. What was left, my sister put in a fold of her robe, and we arose and went home. It would have been impolite to leave behind any of the food given us to eat.

Later in the day Magpie's relatives and friends came to feast on the foods we had taken to Hanging Stone's lodge. Each guest brought a gift, something useful to a new-wed bride—beaded work, fawn-skin work bag, girl's leggings, belt, blanket, woman's robe, calico for a dress, and the like. In the evening two women of Magpie's family brought these gifts to my father's lodge, packing them each in a blanket on her back. They piled the gifts on the floor beside Red Blossom, the elder of my two mothers.

Red Blossom spent the next few days helping me build and decorate the couch that was to mark off the part of our lodge set apart for my husband and me. We even made and placed before the couch a fine, roomy lazyback, or willow chair.

All being now ready, Red Blossom said to me: "Go and call your husband. Go and sit beside him and say, 'I want you to come to my father's lodge.' Do not feel shy. Go boldly and have no fear."

So with my sister I slowly walked to Hanging Stone's lodge. There were several besides the family within, for they were expecting me; but no one said anything as we entered.

Magpie was sitting on his couch, for this in the daytime was used as white men use a lounge or a big chair. My sister and I went over and sat beside him. Magpie smiled and said, "What have you come for?"

"I have come to call you," I answered.

"*Sukkeets*—good!" he said.

Cold Medicine and I arose and returned to my father's lodge. Magpie followed us a few minutes later; for young men did not walk through the village with their sweethearts in the daytime. We should have thought that foolish.

And so I was wed.

I CRIED BUT IT DID NOT DO ANY GOOD
MOUNTAIN WOLF WOMAN WINNEBAGO

In one of her notes to the text of Mountain Wolf Woman, *Nancy Oestreich Lurie wrote: "Among the Winnebago, marriage was a purely secular contract symbolized in the exchange of goods between the couple's parents . . . A larger amount was given by the groom's family, and the wealth of goods was a measure of esteem in which they held the daughter-in-law."*

I was going to be married. I cried but it did not do any good. What would my crying avail me? They had already arranged it. As they were telling me about it my mother said, "My little daughter, I prize you highly. You alone are the youngest child. I prize you highly but nothing can be done about this matter. It is your brothers' doing. You must do whatever your brothers say. If you do not do so, you are going to embarrass them. They have been drinking again, but if you do not do this they will be disgraced. They might even experience something unfortunate."[1] Thus mother spoke to me. She rather frightened me.

My father said, "My little daughter, you do not have very many things to wear, but you will go riding on your little pony. You do not have anything, but you will not walk there." I had a little horse, a dapple-gray kind of pony that was about three years old. Father brought it for me and there the pony stood. They dressed me. I wore a ribbon embroidery skirt and I wore one as a shawl. I wore a heavily beaded binding for the braid of hair down my back, and I had on earrings. It looked as if I were going to a dance. That man was sitting nearby. He started out leading the pony and I followed after. When we reached a road that had high banks on the side, he mounted the horse and I got on behind him. That is the way he brought me home. We rode together. That is how I became a daughter-in-law.

[1] To go against their wishes would be to dishonor them. A misfortune could occur. [This was a strong social control mechanism.—J. K.]

As a daughter-in-law I arrived. When I arrived, he had me go in the wigwam and I went in and sat down. They told me to sit on the bed and I sat there. I took off all the clothing that I was wearing when I got there. I took it all off. I laid down a shawl and whatever I had, all the finery, I put on it: beads, the necklaces, clothing, even the blouse that I was wearing. Finally, the man's mother came in. Outside the wigwam there were canvas-covered wigwams standing here and there. The woman took the things and left. There were women sitting all about outside. They were his female relatives. They divided the things among themselves. As they distributed the things around, everybody contributed something in return. Two or three days from the time of my arrival they took me back with four horses and a double shawl so full of things they could barely tie the corners together. They took me home and later I received two more horses . . . That is how they used to arrange things for young women in the past. They made the girls marry into whatever family they decided upon. They made the arrangements. That is the way they used to do.

At the time my mother was combing my hair, I was weeping at the prospect of becoming a daughter-in-law. She told me, "Daughter, I prize you very much, but this matter cannot be helped. When you are older and know better, you can marry whomever you yourself think that you want to marry." Mother said that to me and I did not forget it![2]

[2] Mountain Wolf Woman was so angry about the marriage arranged for her that she vowed that her children would choose their own mates, which they did.

4.

MARRIAGE IS A SWEET THING WHEN PEOPLE LOVE EACH OTHER

I'M A LITTLE WOMAN WHO'S HAPPY TO SLAVE
KIBKARJUK CARIBOU ESKIMO

Danish ethnologist Knud Rasmussen collected the songs and lore of a number of Eskimo tribes in the 1920s. In his Report of the Fifth Thule Expedition, 1921–1924, *he wrote of Kibkarjuk, an elderly woman. Although her husband Igjugarjuk had thrown her over in favor of a young and pretty woman, she continued to serve him. She told Rasmussen of the time she dragged herself across the frozen wasteland in search of food for Igjugarjuk and the village. She sang of the "great wolf," a tribute to her husband's "song cousin," to please Igjugarjuk. This translation is by Tom Lowenstein.*

I'm only a little woman,
who's happy to slave,
happy to toil.
Anxious to be useful,
I pluck willow flowers
that remind me
of the great wolf's beard.

I wear holes in my kamiks
when I walk far out

to pluck the willow flowers,
that bring to mind
the great wolf's beard,
the great wolf's beard.

WHEN I MARRIED EVERYTHING WAS ALL RIGHT
DELFINA CUERO DIEGUEÑO

After their migration to Baja California, the Diegueño continued their regular visits to the mountains and seashore for seasonal foods. But since they lost their own valley planting lands, some men raised cattle and worked for ranchers and farmers in the area when they could. These recollections of the traditional life-style are from the Autobiography of Delfina Cuero.

When I married, everything was all right; Sebastian was a good man. He worked hard. Sometimes he raised cattle and sold it. Sometimes he went all over looking for work. He worked different places, whatever someone wanted done. That's how we lived over there. . . .

He took care of the children. He took care of my grandfather and grandmother. Oh! Oh! He was good! I had no trouble with him. He took care of me and we always had some food to eat . . .

My husband used to hunt a lot. He was a good hunter for deer. We would use some of the meat and some we would trade for sugar and flour and coffee. Sometimes I would gather medicines and herbs and trade them off for food. We had enough food then with both of us bringing in everything we could find. . . .

We didn't understand money then; the only thing we did was to trade for food or cloth. Sometimes we were lucky and found a

Delfina Cuero (K^wal). Photograph courtesy Mrs. Florence Shipek.

her mark

lot of honey and we could trade that for a cow or a calf to raise. I hunted for greens and roots and seeds as I had been taught. We used some honey for ourselves. We used everything available for food . . . the women dug clams and looked for all different kinds of shell food and plants that grew near the sea while the men fished. We opened up the shells and dried the meat on the rocks in the sun. The children helped their mothers, even with pounding abalone. Some Indians made necklaces of shells, but we didn't. We always needed more food; we were poor and never had time for necklaces. I don't know how to make those things now, only how to find food.

We spent the winters at Ha-a. There were acorns there. We gathered them right near where we lived. Then when things began to grow in the spring, Sebastian and the other Indian men would go to the low mountains on the edge of the desert for about a week. They gathered agave, dug large pits, and roasted the agave in the pits. They used wooden shovels that they had made from mesquite.

The agave gathering and roasting was men's work. Hunting game for meat and hunting for bees and honey were men's jobs also. The women hunted for wild greens, seeds, and fruit. The whole family helped with gathering acorns and pine nuts.

THE WOMEN KNOW AS MUCH AS THE MEN
SARAH WINNEMUCCA HOPKINS PAIUTE

After her marriage to a white man, Lt. L. H. Hopkins of the U.S. Army, Ms. Hopkins remained devoted to her people. She went on the lecture circuit, detailing events in Paiute history and seeking support for the tribe's claims against the government. This description of the role of Paiute women in tribal affairs is from her autobiography, Life Among the Piutes.

The chief's tent is the largest tent, and it is the council-tent, where everyone goes who wants advice. In the evenings the head men go there to discuss everything, for the chiefs do not rule like tyrants; they discuss everything with their people, as a father would in his family. Often they sit up all night. They discuss the doings of all, if they need to be advised. If a boy is not doing well, they talk that over, and if the women are interested, they can share in the talks. If there is not room enough inside, they all go out of doors and make a great circle. The men are in the inner circle, for there would be too much smoke for the women inside. The men never talk without smoking first. The women sit behind them in another circle, and if the children wish to hear, they can be there too.

The women know as much as the men do, and their advice is often asked. We have a republic as well as you. The council-tent is our Congress, and anybody can speak who has anything to say, women and all. They are always interested in what their husbands are doing and thinking about. And they take some part even in the wars. They are always near at hand when fighting is going on, ready to snatch their husbands up and carry them off if wounded or killed. . . .

It means something when the women promise their fathers to make their husbands *themselves*. They faithfully keep with them in all the dangers they can share. They not only take care of their children together, but they do everything together; and when they grow blind, which I am sorry to say is very common, for the smoke they live in destroys their eyes at last, they take sweet care of one another. Marriage is a sweet thing when people love each other. If women could go into your Congress, I think justice would soon be done to the Indians.

SONG OF THE REJECTED WOMAN
KIBKARJUK CARIBOU ESKIMO

Eskimo women only rarely hunted with their husbands, according to Rasmussen. They said that they were afraid that "the great animals would be offended and go away from our shores." They kept house for their men, and chanted the incantations required for success in the hunt. In this song translated by Tom Lowenstein, Kibkarjuk recalled happier days when, as her husband's favorite wife, she had been allowed to hunt caribou.

Inland,
far inland go my thoughts,
my mournful thoughts.
To never leave the woman's bench
is too much to endure:
I want to wander inland,
far inland.
  Ija-je-ja.

My thoughts return
to hunting:
animals, delightful food!
To never leave the woman's bench
is too much to endure:
I want to wander inland,
far inland.
  Ija-je-ja.

I hunted like the men:
I carried weapons,
shot a reindeer[1] bull,
a reindeer cow and calf,

[1] The translator substituted the word *reindeer* for *caribou* "for reasons of rhythm."

yes, slew them with my arrows,
with my arrows,
one evening toward winter,
as the sky-dusk fell
far inland.
  Ija-je-ja.

This is what I think about,
this is what I struggle with,
while inland, under falling snow,
the earth turns white,
far inland.
  Ija-je-ja.

I SAID . . . I AM GOING HOME
MARIA CHONA PAPAGO

Ms. Chona was married to a shaman, a person of great prestige in Papago society. "For a shaman to have more than one wife was standard custom . . ." comments Ruth Underhill in her introduction to Autobiography of a Papago Woman, *"But Chona resented her co-wife. The result was a minor rebellion, soon settled."*

One day I went with my little girl to buy meat at a neighbor's house where they had just butchered. I came back and, under our arbor, there sat a girl. The relative that lived next door to us called over and said: "My elder sister, your husband's married."

Most men did not take two wives with us then, but the medicine men always did. In fact, they took four. But I had never thought my husband would do it. You see, we married so young, even before I had really become a maiden. It was as if we had been children in the same house. I had grown fond of him. We starved so much together.

The other woman spoke to me. "I see you're his wife. You had better take care of him. It's not my fault." I knew that. I knew they brought her over to our house just the way my mother brought me. Perhaps she did not know he had a wife till I came back from buying meat. I said: "I know it isn't your fault. But I am going home."

I piled my clothes in a basket, and I put in a large butcher knife. I thought if he followed, I would kill him. Then I took my little girl and went away. It was late evening. I went to the house of a relative and asked to stay the night, and early before morning stands up, I got up to walk to Mesquite Root, across the valley. Before I started, my husband came. He stood there and looked at us and he said to my little girl: "What will you do, go with your mother?" "Yes." He said: "Go on. I'll come to see you sometimes." He thought it was a joke.

In the afternoon I got to Mesquite Root and told my brother. He said: "All right."

Next day we were all in the field, eating watermelons, and there my husband came. My brother said: "What do you want?" "I just came after these people." My brother was angry. My husband said: "Her father came and proposed to me for her. It seemed a good thing." He meant that woman. But my brother sent him away and so he went. I did not say anything. I thought my husband would send away that woman and come back.

A few days later my uncle found out. He said: "We cannot have this woman here with no one to care for her. We must find a husband. We must show that other man that he cannot get her back." So he went to an old man and proposed for me. That old man was the one who had danced me when I became a maiden. He had had a wife then, but now she was dead and he was living alone. He was a rich man; he had horses.

He was a distant relative of ours, one whom I called my elder brother. My father would not have allowed me to be offered to him, for we do not marry relatives. When my brother spoke to him, he said: "Very well, my younger brother. I will be there in two days."

My brother and my uncle came and told my mother and me. I

cried. My mother said: "Wait. Her husband will be sorry and come for her. They have been together since they were young." But my brother would not: "Mother, you'll see. This man may be old, but he has something. He may take care of her and of you, too. That's one of my reasons." You see, my family was poor then.

I did not say anything. No woman has a right to speak against her brother, even if he is younger, as this one was. And my mother had no right either, against the men. My brother said to me: "Look here, he has something. He may be a help to you and to me." I knew that my family was poor. I said: "I'll see. If this man is good to me, I'll stay. If not, I'll give it up."

In two days the old man came, in the evening, on a horse. My brother spoke to him as if he was that old man's father: "If you don't take care of her, I'll take her back." The old man said: "All right." Then he told me: "I'll try to take good care of you, feed you, and give you all you don't have. Now you go to sleep. Early in the morning I'll come and get you." He came and took me behind him on a horse and we went down the valley to Where the Rock Stands Up. My little girl stayed with my mother. . . .

That old man had many horses. He traded them to the Apaches, and they paid him money, not food and clothes, as my first husband used to be paid. He could go to Tucson and buy any kind of food he wanted, lard and wheat and potatoes and cow's meat. I got fat. I could not stoop over to put on those new shoes. My uncle came to see us when he was trading horses and he said: "What have you been feeding her?"

But I felt bad. I did not love that old man. I was not fond of him. I used to go in the washes and lie flat under the greasewood bushes and cry. Or I would lie on the floor in the house, when my husband was away, covered up with blankets. It hurt.

I never saw my first husband again. They told me that when he heard of my new marriage he cried. He said: "I didn't think she would take my child from me. I thought she would stay near and at last come back."

SONGS OF DIVORCE
JANE GREEN OJIBWE (CHIPPEWA)

It was an Ojibwe custom, according to Frances Densmore: "If a woman quarreled with her husband and was sent away, she gave a dance in about three days" and her husband did the same. These songs of divorce were recorded by Jane Green, an Ojibwe woman from the Skeena River country in British Columbia, and were translated by Densmore in Music of the Indians of British Columbia.

I guess you love me now.
I guess you admire me now.
You threw me away like something that tasted bad.
You treat me as if I were a rotten fish.

I thought you were good at first.
I thought you were like silver and I find you are like lead.
You see me high up.
I walk through the sun.
I am like the sunlight myself.

5.

THE GREAT SEA SETS ME ADRIFT

LOVE-CHARM SONG
OJIBWE (CHIPPEWA)

Mysticism and spirituality permeated every aspect of tribal life. Among the Ojibwe "the love-charm song was a popular form of magic," wrote Frances Densmore who recorded songs of the sacred medicine society on the Red Lake Reservation. Densmore persuaded a wizened, sixty-year-old woman to sing one song. She did so in a secluded place where no one else could hear her, then said it meant that she was as beautiful as the roses.

I can charm the man
He is completely fascinated
by me.

Niwawin′gawia′ . . .
Ĕnĭ′nĭwa′ . . .

THE PEOPLES WHO STAND UPON THIS EARTH . . . WHITE BUFFALO WOMAN OGLALA SIOUX

According to the Oglala holy man, Black Elk, White Buffalo Woman appeared to the Sioux people enveloped in a cloud. When it lifted, she articulated a world view that became the basis of their religion. Her words are recorded by Joseph Epes Brown in his book The Sacred Pipe: Black Elk's Account of the Seven Rites of the Oglala Sioux.

All of this [creation] is sacred, and so do not forget. Every dawn as it comes is a holy event, and every day is holy, for the light comes from your Father Wakan-Tanka;[1] and also you must always remember that the two-leggeds and all the other peoples who stand upon this earth are sacred and should be treated as such.

SONG TO EARTH MOTHER ZUÑI

Perhaps because they viewed the menstrual cycle as a sign of impurity, most desert tribes restricted the role of women in priestly functions. A Papago woman could not be a shaman; a Zuñi woman could aspire to that role only by inheritance. Prayer sticks—feathered fertility symbols considered the most sacred of gifts to the gods—could be offered by Zuñi women, but were made only by men. But in their ritual poetry the Zuñi poured out their reverence for the "earth mother," and endowed her with life and spirit.

. . . That our earth mother may wrap herself
In a fourfold robe of white meal;

[1] *Wakan-Tanka:* a great, mysterious supernatural force that the Sioux honored with the yearly Sun Dance.

That she may be covered with frost flowers;
That yonder on all the mossy mountains,
The forests may huddle together with the cold;
That their arms may be broken by the snow,
In order that the land may be thus,
I have made my prayer sticks into living beings . . .

All over the land
May the flesh of our earth mother
Crack open from the cold;
That your thoughts may bend to this,
That your words may be to this end;
For this with prayers I send you forth.

When our earth mother is replete with living waters,
When spring comes, . . .
Then from wherever the rainmakers stay quietly,
They will send forth their misty breath;
Their massed clouds filled with water will come out to
  sit down with us;
Far from their homes,
With outstretched hands of water they will embrace the corn,
Stepping down to caress them with their fresh waters,
With their fine rain caressing the earth,
With their heavy rain caressing the earth . . .

The clay-lined hollows of our earth mother
Will overflow with water,
From all the lakes
Will rise the cries of the children of the rainmakers,
In all the lakes
There will be joyous dancing. . . .

HELP PEOPLES
SANAPIA COMANCHE

Sanapia, the last surviving Comanche medicine woman or "Eagle Doctor," was born in 1895 in a tipi at Fort Sill, Oklahoma. From her mother, a medicine woman, she received instruction in the use of medicinal plants, as well as in the ethical responsibilities of a doctor. From the eagle, her guardian spirit, she was believed to have received supernatural powers. Her grandmother gave Sanapia her seal of approval and blessing. Sanapia recalled the experience in Sanapia: Comanche Medicine Woman.

I was pretty good size, about fourteen I guess . . . she put cedar on them coals and she pray and sing. Then she put her hand on my head and I inhale that cedar and she fan it on my legs and arms, all over my body. She would sing a song and she prayed . . .

> You, I don't know what you are, but I want you to bless this little girl so she can grow up and live to be an old lady like me. You, the one who go in the night and watch people, I don't know who you are, but you're like that, bless her. And this earth, I want her to walk on you for many, many years. I want her to be strong and healthy and I want her to live many years.

And after she got through, she took that red paint and put water in it and . . . smeared it all on my face, and rubbed it from my knees down to the bottom of my feet. Then she said:

> This paint comes from the earth and she's going to stand on it. And she's going to live long life after she gets old. Help peoples. And when she gets real old, and her hair turns gray and white and her teeth fall out, well, that's when she's going to die.

That's what she told me.

I GOT THE POWER IN MY HANDS
SANAPIA COMANCHE

Sanapia's "medicine" has been likened to psychogenic healing. It contains elements of traditional Plains Indian mysticism, Peyotism, and Christianity, all of which were practiced by members of her family.

I was doctoring my niece one time . . . She had cancer and liver. So the doctor, white doctor, gave up. . . . Somebody came to our house that afternoon and told us that L—— was dying. . . . When we got there she was just lying on her back . . . nobody was in the house except her. Her husband was gone and her children were all gone. She was white as a sheet. Her face was just white and her lips were blue. She didn't even notice me come in. I wake her up and said, "Are you sleeping? What's the matter with you?" She said, "I'm . . . going to die tonight. That's what the doctor told me. They dismissed me from the hospital . . . Could you help me?"

That's what she said. And I told J——, "You go get your brothers. I'll get her out of it . . . That cancer ain't nothing to me." And he beat it down there to his brothers and they come in right after dark. That night we soaked that deer hide . . . soaked it in water till it could get soft, and they put it on the drum. And right there in the middle of town . . . I said, "Let's have this peyote meeting for her tonight . . . drum all night. Let me fix her up. She be all right."

And so that night we had a drumming right there in the middle of town. And she was worse the next morning. . . . That night we had another peyote meeting inside of the house and it was just pouring down rain and we had the meeting for her. Took that peyote and said, "Our fathers, way back in years . . . our grandfathers took this medicine, and they said that whenever anybody sick like that, you just take this and chew it and then put it in your hands and let her swallow it . . . give her four at the start." And I done that. I prayed and talked to that peyote just like I'm talking to you. I said, "If you don't get her well, I don't want you. If you not nothing, if you ain't got power, I don't want to use you anymore."

God made me in this world and he gave me this power just like when he was here on land. Jesus went around blessing people and healing the sick and everything like that, and I believe that I got the power in my hands. I believe I could get her well. So that night we had a peyote meeting and the second night we had another one and the fourth night . . . the fourth night she died. She just went out. She was blue . . . fingernails were blue and her lips turn blue. I told them, "Take that drum hide out." And they took it, rinse it out, squeeze it, and I said, "Give it to me." And I put it on her head. I rub her face with it, and four times I done that to her and then I sing my medicine song. When anybody's dying and I doctor them, that's the only time I sing that special song I got. So I said, "You all carry her and put her on my bed," and they carried her. I said, "You all stay out there in the front room." And they all stayed out there and it was still pouring rain. Everybody get out. It was raining out there and the wind was howling around. I sing this song and I fan her and I doctor her . . . give her that medicine. I don't know how many times I give her that. And after a while she open her eyes and said, "I'm sure thirsty." And after that she got all right.

DREAM SONG OF A WOMAN
PAPAGO

The Papago woman was not permitted to play an active role in the ceremonial life of her community. But songmaking was an accepted outlet for a woman, in fact, a requirement for success in life, as Ruth Underhill wrote in her book Papago Music.

Where the mountain crosses
On top of the mountain
  I do not myself know where.

I wandered where my mind and my heart
Seemed to be lost.
  I wandered away.

I MOVE TOWARD A GOOD WAY
MOUNTAIN WOLF WOMAN WINNEBAGO

The Peyote Cult, which spread to the Plains and Woodland tribes in the 1880s, involved eating the part of the peyote cactus plant that induced hallucinations, and solemn rituals. It incorporated ancient Plains Indian supernaturalism with Christian symbolism. Some viewed consumption of peyote as a form of communion, but there were wide differences in practice. In her autobiography, Mountain Wolf Woman told how peyote altered her life.

I was once a Christian. Then, when we went to Nebraska, I ate peyote which is even a Christian way. Three things I did.[2] But peyote alone is the best. I learned very many things.

Whatever is good, that I would do. Whatever is good to say, that I would say. These people are good to live with. I was respected among these people. I moved toward a good way. I thought that was a good thing, that I would be strengthened. That is the way I am. I pray to God. I always ask of him that I move toward a good way, that my children and my grandchildren and the people live well. I was strengthened. Today I am in good health. I continue to live happily. I pray for the sick. I pray for the dead. Whatever good I can say, that I say. That is the way I

[2] As a young woman she was initiated into the Winnebago "Medicine Lodge," later became a Christian, and, finally, a Peyotist.

Mountain Wolf Woman. Photograph by Speltz Studio, Black River Falls, Wisconsin.

always try to be. If anyone says anything to me, I always say good of him, then nothing he is saying can hurt me. That is what I do. That is the way I am.

I am old, but though I am seventy-three years old my body is strong. I make my own clothing. There are women living here and there today who are younger than I am who are helplessly infirm. I am able to move about. Where I live I care for myself. My children sometimes say they would take care of me. "Wait a while," I say, "until I am older. You can take care of me when I can no longer take care of myself." I always say I am happy the way I am and that I hope to continue in that fashion. If I am good to people, after while, when my life ends, I expect to go to heaven. I say no more.

A WOMAN SHAMAN'S SONG
UVAVNUK IGLULIK ESKIMO

In his Report of the Fifth Thule Expedition, 1921–1924, *Knud Rasmussen wrote of a ceremony he attended in a domed snowhouse. The woman shaman, Uvavnuk, chanted this song to call up her helping spirit. Then, all present began to recite their misdeeds and, as though purified, made gestures as if to cast off evil. Once again, a Tom Lowenstein translation.*

The great sea stirs me.
The great sea sets me adrift.
It sways me like the weed
on a river-stone.

The sky's height stirs me.
The strong wind blows through my mind.
It carries me with it,
so I shake with joy.

6.

THE DEAD DANCE WITH THE LIVING

IN THE SPIRIT-LAND
SARAH WINNEMUCCA HOPKINS PAIUTE

In Life Among the Piutes, *Ms. Hopkins contrasted the Paiute view of death with the hellfire-and-damnation doctrine preached by Christian zealots she had been exposed to.*

[We] believe that in the Spirit-land those that die still watch over those that are living. When I was a child in California, I heard the Methodist minister say that everybody that did wrong was burned in hell forever. I was so frightened it made me very sick. He said the blessed ones in heaven looked down and saw their friends burning and could not help them. I wanted to be unborn, and cried so that my mother and the others told me it was not so, that it was only here that people did wrong and were in the hell that it made, and that those that were in the Spirit-land saw us here and were sorry for us. But we should go to them when we died, where there was never any wrongdoing, and so no hell. That is our religion.

OWL WOMAN'S DEATH SONG
PAPAGO

In The Winged Serpent *Margot Astrov wrote: "To the Indian . . . earth and tree and stone and the wide scope of the heaven were tenanted with numberless supernaturals and the wandering souls of the dead. And it was only in the solitude of remote places and in the sheltering silence of the night that the voices of these spirits might be heard." This song is from Ruth Underhill's* Papago Music.

In the great night my heart will go out,
Toward me the darkness comes rattling,
In the great night my heart will go out.

PRAYER OF A MOTHER WHOSE CHILD HAS DIED
KWAKIUTL

According to Franz Boas who studied the Kwakiutl of British Columbia, a firstborn child was doted on. If the child sickened and died, its mother carried it in her arms. Then all the women came to visit and wail with her; soon the mother began to speak:

Ah, ah, ah! What is the reason, child, that you have done this to me? I have tried hard to treat you well when you came to me to have me for your mother. Look at all your toys. What is the reason that you desert me, child? May it be that I did something, child, to you in the way I treated you, child? I will try better when you come back to me, child. Please, only become at once well in the place to which you are going. As soon as you are made well, please, come back to me, child. Please, do not stay away there. Please, only have mercy on me who is your mother, child.

THE WIDOW'S SONG
QERNERTOQ COPPER ESKIMO

Of the spirit hymns of the Copper Eskimo, Knud Rasmussen wrote that they "are sung in the festival house to Hilap inue, *spirits of the air, who assist mankind. Words and tunes have been handed down for generations . . . The words are vague . . . they act by the force of their fantasy." Tom Lowenstein is the translator.*

Why will people
have no mercy on me?
Sleep comes hard
since Maula's killer
showed no mercy.
Ijaja-ijaja.

Was the agony I felt so strange,
when I saw the man I loved
thrown on the earth
with bowed head?
Murdered by enemies,
worms have forever
deprived him
of his homecoming.
Ijaja-ijaja.

He was not alone
in leaving me.
My little son
has vanished
to the shadow-land.
Ijaja-ijaja.

Now I'm like a beast
caught in the snare

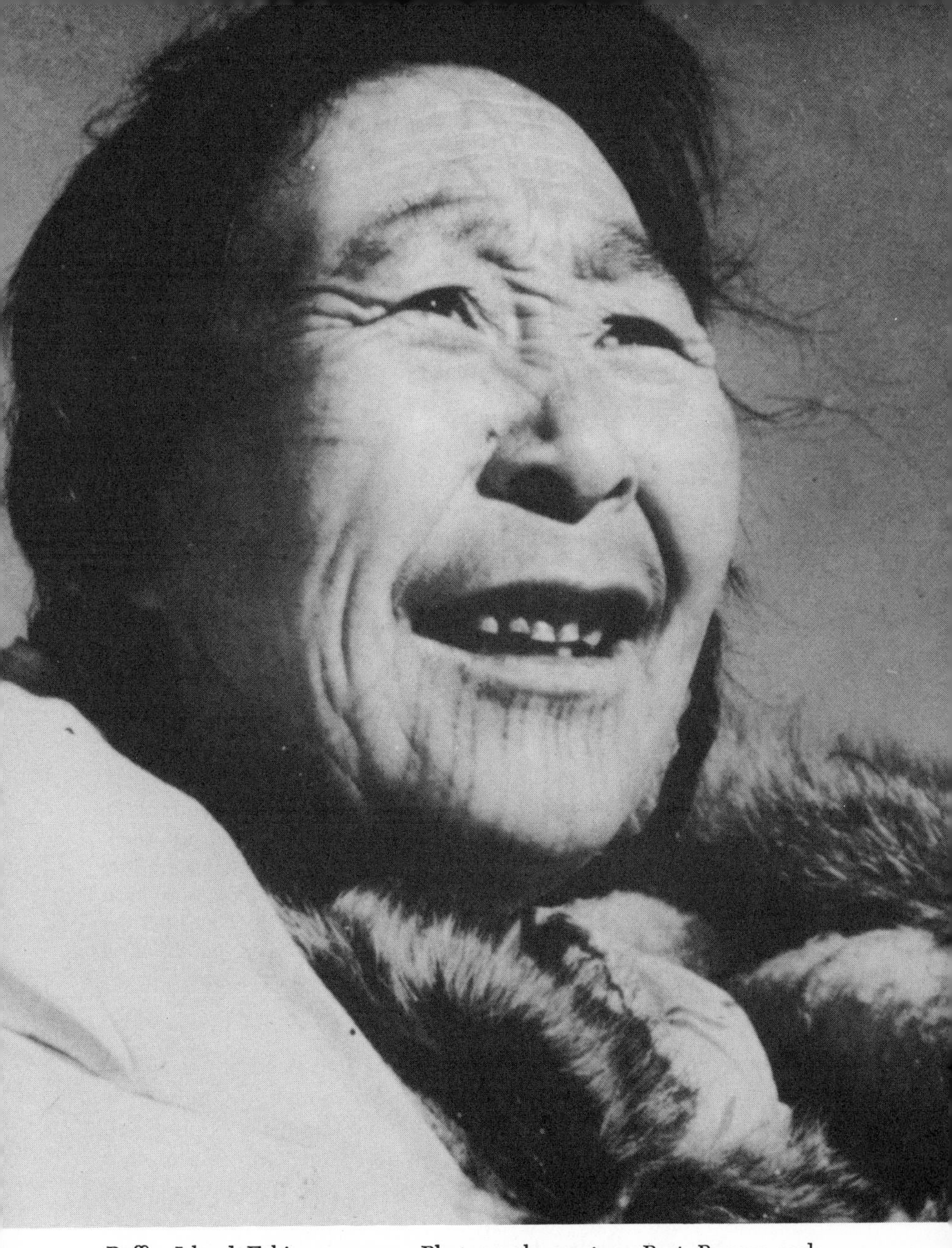

Baffin Island Eskimo woman. Photograph courtesy Bert Beaver and National Film Board of Canada.

of my hut.
Ijaja-ijaja.

Long will be my journey
on the earth.
It seems as if
I'll never get beyond
the footprints that I make.

A worthless amulet
is all my property:
while the northern light
dances its sparkling steps
in the sky.

THEY WOULD NOT LET ME SEE HIM, MY HUSBAND
LINA ZUNI ZUÑI

Among the Zuñi of New Mexico there was a belief that the spirits of the dead mingled with the invisible forces of nature. After a death, there was a period of intense mourning, followed by recital of a ritual formula and an offering to sacred ancestors. Prayer was thought to have a healing function, as well as to protect the bereaved person from the haunting influence of the dead soul. For her Zuñi Texts, *published in 1926, translator Ruth Bunzel interviewed pueblo residents, one of whom, Lina Zuni, was then seventy years old.*

They came. They brought the ones who had been killed by the white people. My aunts were with me. My mother, my father, my aunts, held me and went with me. I came there; I was pregnant. They would not let me see him, my husband. Only my mother saw him. She told me. It was not good. . . . So they buried them in the graveyard, just before sunset.

. . . My grandfather took care of me. "It is very dangerous; you must fast. You must drink medicine. You must vomit. It is very dangerous. No one may touch you. It is very dangerous, you must fast. No one must touch you. You must stay alone. You must sit alone in the corner. Only your little boy may hold you. No one must touch you." Grandfather gathered medicine for me. This he soaked. He mixed it in a fine bowl. He brewed medicine. "This you will drink. You will vomit," he said to me. I was very wretched. This was very dangerous. When it was still early, when the sun had not yet risen, my grandfather took me far away. We scattered prayer meal. Here in the left hand I had black prayer meal, and here the right kind of prayer meal. When we had gone far I passed it four times over my head and scattered it. One should not speak. Again with this, I sprinkled prayer meal with a prayer:

My fathers,
Our Sun Father.
Our mother, Dawn,
Coming out standing to your sacred place,
Somewhere we shall pass you on your road.
This from which we form our flesh,
The white corn,
Prayer meal,
Shell,
Corn pollen,
I offer to you.
To the Sun who is our father,
To you I offer it
To you, I offer prayer meal.
To you, I offer corn pollen.
According to the words of my prayer,
So may it be.
May there be no deviation.
Sincerely from my heart I send forth my prayers.
To you, prayer meal, shell, I offer.
Corn pollen I offer.
According to the words of my prayer,
So may it be.

I would sprinkle prayer meal. I would inhale from the prayer meal. I would sprinkle the right kind of prayer meal. . . .

All alone I sat. I did not eat meat, nor salt, nor grease. I fasted from meat. It was very dangerous. Much my aunt, my grandfather exhorted me. When I was young, they said to me, "Fortunate you are to be alive. Sometimes you will be happy because of something. Sometimes you will be sorrowful. You will cry. This kind of person you shall be. You are fortunate to be alive." . . . And just so I have lived. . . . If one's husband dies one will not sleep. She will lie down as if she sleeps, and when sleep overcomes her she will sleep. But after a little while she will wake, and will not sleep. She will cry, she will be lonely. She will not care to eat. She will take thought of what to do and where to go. When a child or a relative dies, one cries for them properly. Husband and wife talk together to relieve their thoughts. Then they will forget their trouble. But when one's husband dies there is no happiness. . . .

It was very dangerous. It was the same as when an enemy dies, it was very dangerous. Four mornings I vomited. And so many days I sprinkled prayer meal far off, four times. And so many days I fasted. I was still a young woman . . .

For one year I would cry. I was thoughtful for my old husband. Then father spoke with me. Then I was happy. I did not worry. My uncle desired it for me. "It is all right, niece. Do not cry. It cannot be helped. It is ever thus. Do not think of where you have come from, but rather look forward to where you are to go."

A WOMAN'S SONG FOR HER DROWNED BROTHER TLINGIT

Perhaps he went into the sun's trail
So that I can never see him again.

7.

NO ONE CARES FOR OUR CORN SONGS NOW

MY POOR PEOPLE DIED OFF VERY FAST
SARAH WINNEMUCCA HOPKINS PAIUTE

In 1877–1878 the Paiutes joined with the Bannock tribe in a war to resist white encroachment on their hunting lands. After their defeat, they were forcibly removed to the Yakima Reservation in Washington. Ms. Hopkins, interpreter for the United States Army, served also as spokeswoman for her people. She protested this disruption of their lives. This episode in Paiute history is from Life Among the Piutes.

We traveled all day. It snowed all day long. We camped, and that night a woman became a mother; and during the night the baby died, and was put under the snow. The next morning the mother was put into the wagon. She was almost dead when we went into camp. That night she too was gone, and left on the roadside, her poor body not even covered with the snow.

In five days, three more children were frozen to death, and another woman became a mother. Her child lived three days, but the mother died. We then crossed Columbia River . . .

We arrived in Yakima on the last day of the month. . . . we were turned over to Father Wilbur and his civilized Indians, as he called them . . . as if we were so many horses or cattle . . . They did not come because they loved us, or because they were Christians. No; they were just like all civilized people; they came to take us up there because they were to be paid for it. They had a kind of shed made to put us in. You know what kind of shed you make for your stock in wintertime . . . How we did suffer with cold. There was no wood, and the snow was waist-deep, and many died off just as cattle or horses do after traveling so long in the cold.

Now came the working time. My people were set to work clearing land; both men and women went to work and boys too. They cleared sixty acres of land for wheat. They had it all cleared in about ten days . . .

We had the finest wheat that was ever raised on the reservation, for my people pulled out all the cockle and smut. . . . I am sorry to say that Father Wilbur kept our wheat for his white friends and gave us the bad wheat, and the bad wheat was ground just as you would grind it for your hogs. The bad flour made us all sick. My poor people died off very fast. At first Father Wilbur and his Christian Indians told us we could bury our dead in their graveyard; but they soon got tired of us, and said we could not bury them there anymore.

WE DO NOT WANT ANY OTHER HOME
CELSA APAPAS CUPEÑO

Despite the objections of tribal members the tiny Cupeño tribe, which in 1910 numbered not more than 200 people, was removed from its mountainous villages in southern California to San Diego County. Celsa Apapas was one of those who spoke out against the move.

You asked us to think what place we like next best to this place, where we always lived. You see that graveyard out there? There

On the beach—Chinook. Edward S. Curtis, 1910.

are our fathers and our grandfathers. You see that Eagle-nest Mountain and that Rabbit-hole Mountain? When God made them, He gave us this place. We have always been here. We do not care for any other place—If you give us the best place in the world, it is not so good for us as this—This is our home—We cannot live anywhere else. We were born here and our fathers are buried here—We want this place and not any other. . . .

There is no other place for us. We do not want you to buy any other place. If you will not buy this place, we will go into the mountains like quail, and die there, the old people and the women and children. Let the Government be glad and proud. It can kill us. We do not fight. We do what it says. If we cannot live here, we want to go into the mountains and die. We do not want any other home.

I WONDERED WHAT THE SPIRIT THOUGHT

PITSEOLAK ASHOONA CAPE DORSET ESKIMO

As a young woman, Pitseolak married Ashoona, an inland hunter who brought her many caribou- and sealskins. She sewed and picked berries on the tundra. Her life story, told when she was in her seventies, contrasts old ways and new.

We used to eat seal, whale, caribou, ducks, and ptarmigan all raw, though we used to cook the goose, and . . . the polar bear . . . Sometimes in the winter it was boring in the igloo but we never stayed inside much. We had warmer clothes in those days, and it used to be fun when it was windy . . . when we felt happy in camp, Ashoona and I would play the accordion . . . The little children would come and dance . . .

I think the new times started for the Eskimos after the white people's war, when the white men began to make many houses in the Arctic. Eskimos began to move into the settlements, and then the white people started helping us to get these houses. That's why life changed. I don't think everybody was too fond of moving from the camps, but they still came . . . They are working for the white man now . . .

In some ways I like living in a warm house, but in the old days, before all these things happened, we were always healthy. I was never sick, not even with all the children I had. In these late years I have been sick most of the time and I have felt each year harder to bear. Now that we all live in one place we get sick a lot . . .

I think the new ways would be better than the old, except that nowadays the young people make so much trouble. A long time ago when I was bringing up my children, they would do what you told them to do. If you gave them something to eat, they were grateful and happy about it . . . Now, all that has changed. They don't listen at all. People get worse when they all live in one place. The young people are always in trouble . . .

I heard there is someone–not a human being but a spirit–in the moon. When I heard that the two men had landed on the moon, I wondered what the spirit thought of these two men landing on his land . . .

I CANNOT FORGET OUR OLD WAYS
WAHEENEE HIDATSA

Almost eighty years old when she told her life story, Waheenee was conservative, clinging to native beliefs and longing for the old days. Still, she recognized that the young people had to change and adapt if they were to survive.

I am an old woman now. The buffaloes and blacktail deer are gone, and our Indian ways are almost gone. Sometimes I find it hard to believe that I ever lived them.

My little son grew up in the white man's school. He can read books, and he owns cattle and has a farm. He is a leader among our Hidatsa people, helping teach them to follow the white man's road.

He is kind to me. We no longer live in an earth lodge, but in a house with chimneys; and my son's wife cooks by a stove.

But for me, I cannot forget our old ways.

Often in summer I rise at daybreak and steal out to the cornfields; and as I hoe the corn I sing to it, as we did when I was young. No one cares for our corn songs now.

Sometimes at evening I sit, looking out on the big Missouri. The sun sets, and dusk steals over the water. In the shadows I seem again to see our Indian village, with smoke curling upward from the earth lodges; and in the river's roar I hear the yells of the warriors, the laughter of little children as of old. It is but an old woman's dream. Again I see but shadows and hear only the roar of the river; and tears come into my eyes. Our Indian life, I know, is gone forever.

THE WHITE PEOPLE NEVER CARED FOR LAND
HOLY WOMAN WINTU

The Wintu Indians of California revered and cared for the land, writes anthropologist Dorothy Lee.[1] *They grieved over the destruction caused by the search for gold and by hydraulic mining, which tore huge holes in the earth and left it defoliated. This lament for the land is by an old holy woman of the Wintu.*

The white people never cared for land or deer or bear. When we Indians kill meat, we eat it all up. When we dig roots, we make

[1] "Anthropology," in *Religious Perspectives in College Teaching* edited by Hoxie N. Fairchild, *et al.* Copyright 1952, The Ronald Press Company, New York.

little holes. When we build houses, we make little holes. When we burn grass for grasshoppers, we don't ruin things. We shake down acorns and pine nuts. We don't chop down the trees. We only use dead wood. But the white people plow up the ground, pull down the trees, kill everything. The tree says: "Don't. I am sore. Don't hurt me." But they chop it down and cut it up. The spirit of the land hates them; they blast out trees and stir it up to its depths. They saw up the trees. That hurts them. The Indians never hurt anything, but the white people destroy all. They blast rocks and scatter them on the ground. The rock says: "Don't. You are hurting me." But the white people pay no attention. When the Indians use rocks, they take little round ones for their cooking . . . how can the spirit of the earth like the white man? . . . everywhere the white man has touched it, it is sore.

MY WAY IS GETTING NO GOOD UP TO TODAY
SANAPIA COMANCHE

To some Indian people, the medicine woman Sanapia is a healer, a member of a time-honored Comanche institution. To others she is simply an eccentric old woman. Sanapia views herself as outmoded. David Jones, who interviewed her when she was in her seventies wrote in Sanapia: Comanche Medicine Woman: *"As we sat watching automobiles moving along a highway or observed the skyscrapers, she would speak of the incongruity of herself and the twentieth-century world in which she lives."*

I just can't think how it came this way. Look at them cars. I remember when I never seen them before. And all those white peoples walking along, and those big buildings all around here. I don't like it here. My grandmother said this way would come and now here I am, and she died long time back in years. Maybe I should be with her now because my way is getting no good up to today.

Maybe I should be dead too. Even my own kids growing up like white peoples, and they think I'm just a funny old woman. I know they do! But I ain't got too many more years to go yet. And here you, a white person, asking me all those old ways, and my kids go around here and there and don't even talk to me about those things. It sure is funny, ain't it?

PART II
VOICES OF TODAY

Photograph by Paul Conklin.

I will not allow you to ignore me . . .
I am living.

In the early twentieth century, tribal people were wards of the U.S. government—for the most part they were landless and politically impotent. In 1924 they won citizenship rights, but they had to go to the courts for enforcement. The 1930s saw the restoration of some degree of self-government. Funds were made available for land acquisition and economic development; but this was tokenism and touched few Native Americans. Most remained indigent, victims of the government policy of benign neglect.

Then in the 1950s, the government began a campaign on some reservations to terminate the people's treaty-guaranteed rights to federal protection and social, health, and welfare services, in the interest of encouraging self-sufficiency. But many Indians felt this program was imposed on them before they were ready for it; most reservations are depressed areas, not equipped to assume major financial burdens. In some cases, termination caused severe hardships.

Because of the shortage of jobs on and near reservations, government officials encouraged tribal people to move to the cities. But relocation created more problems than it solved. Transplanted to a technologically oriented environment for which they were unprepared, many Indians were adrift without friends or future. There were government-run job-training programs, but Indians were often relegated to menial positions and were discouraged from having higher aspirations. Services and support systems for the nonreservation Indian were minimal.

Some made the transition. For the most part, Indian women were less restricted by traditional roles than were men. They went to work as domestics and in factories, offices, schools, and hospitals. Perhaps Indian women were less threatening than men to a white populace brought up on the "savage Indian" stereotype. Public assistance kept some families alive. Although scholarships for gifted young people gave some a belief in the future, for too many, the options were few and doors remained closed. They remained on the dole, subservient to the white power structure; resorting to liquor, or suicide, sometimes seemed to be the only way out.

Poverty remains the most persistent problem Indian people

have to contend with. There have been attempts to establish industries on reservations, with varying degrees of success. But the culture and needs of the people are often disregarded. A case in point: a fishhook plant was set up on the Pine Ridge Reservation in South Dakota, second largest in the nation. It was to provide jobs for the reservation work force, more than sixty percent of which was without steady employment.[1] Once daring horsemen and warriors of the plains, Sioux men are sensitive about their image. Tying feathers onto fishhooks was considered women's work, and the men quit.[2] So began again the cycle of joblessness, nonsupport of families, and drinking to assuage feelings of inadequacy.

In depressed areas crime and disease flourish. The number of Indian people imprisoned for drunkenness, vagrancy, assault, and drug offenses is disproportionate to their relationship to the total population. This is in part due to racist attitudes of law enforcement officials. Many Indians are not fully aware of their legal rights and responsibilities. The suicide rate for Native Americans is much higher than that for whites. Statistics affirm widespread infant mortality, more deaths from malnutrition, pneumonia, and tuberculosis, and more permanent damage caused by untreated eye and ear infections than in the general population.

Doctors are being trained. Medicines are dispensed; broken bones are set. But not enough is done to correct the underlying causes of poor health—unsafe housing, improper nutrition and sanitation, or to combat native peoples' distrust of "white man's medicine."[3]

Reservation Indians today often find themselves enveloped in a web of bureaucratic controls collectively known as the Bureau of Indian Affairs (BIA). This agency was originally empowered

[1] Kaplan, Gans, and Cahn, "Description of Pine Ridge," *Oglala Sioux Model Reservation Program* (1968), p. 4, cited in *Our Brother's Keeper,* eds. Edgar J. Cahn and David W. Hearne (New York: New American Library, 1975), p. 2.

[2] Robert Thomas, "Colonialism: Classic and Internal," in *New University Thought,* 55, no. 4 (Winter 1966/1967), pp. 39–43.

[3] Edgar S. Cahn and David W. Hearne, eds., *Our Brother's Keeper: The Indian in White America* (New York: New American Library, 1975), pp. 62–64.

to negotiate peace treaties with sovereign nations. After their defeat, its stated purpose was, in the words of U.S. Commissioner of Indian Affairs Francis Walker, to reduce the Indians "to the condition of supplicants for charity."[4] The BIA was given sweeping powers to govern the conquered Indian territories, which it is hesitant to relinquish.

One of these powers was the right to take Indian youngsters away from their communities to educate them. The BIA boarding school broadened horizons for some, but for many it merely enforced assimilation. Teachers and textbooks disseminated stereotypes that continue to haunt Indian people. Taught to deny their heritage and "be white," many youngsters forgot who they were and became alienated from their people. Today, courses in tribal languages and cultures are helping to restore pride in native traditions. Although the trend is toward desegregation, privately run all-Indian "survival schools" are trying to meet the special needs of Indian youngsters.

Indians often allege that regional offices of the BIA are hampered by inadequate funding and by insensitivity to the needs of the people they are supposed to serve. But Sioux lawyer Vine Deloria, Jr., believes that progress has been made:

> Finally in the 1960s, after nearly a century of neglect, funds began to become available for capital improvements such as tribal buildings, community halls, roads, and housing. The past few years have been the first time there has been money available for development of the reservations . . .[5]

BIA offices are most successful, Deloria claims, when they achieve a partnership with the local residents, funding and supporting tribal programs and enterprises.

The BIA, as trustee of most Indian lands, has presided over the gradual erosion of the tribal land base:

[4] Shirley Hill Witt and Stan Steiner, eds., *The Way* (New York: Vintage Books, 1972), p. 61.

[5] Vine Deloria, Jr., *Custer Died for Your Sins* (New York: The Macmillan Co., 1969), p. 139.

> Between the years 1887 and 1966, the Indian land base has decreased from 138 million acres to 55 million acres. Indian land remains the subject of continual and unrelenting expropriation—most frequently in the name of progress.[6]

Energy companies have moved onto the Navajo Reservation in New Mexico, one of the poorest in the U.S., offering cash payments for land rich in mineral resources. But money will not prevent destruction of the land surface, or damage to animals, plants, and the atmosphere, inevitable byproducts of strip mining and gasification plants. Ignoring the protests of the Indians of Fort Berthold, North Dakota, the Army Corps of Engineers flooded one fourth of their reservation, the most fertile land, at the time of the opening of the Garrison Dam. "Five years after the Indians gave up the lands, a rich oil deposit was discovered. They received no royalties."[7] Tribal land has been taken "for the public good" in New York, Pennsylvania, Maine, Arizona, and elsewhere. Industry is ravaging Alaska's natural wonderland. And so the story of rape of Indian land goes on.

A system entrenched over centuries is not easily changed. The Indian communities do not speak with one voice. The diversity of Indian peoples and the complexity of the political and cultural forces operating within each nation make unity difficult to attain. Activists believe the white community must be prodded into reform. But some Indians find the violence that often accompanies demonstrations self-destructive.

Many Native Americans are working quietly within the system to bring about change. Organizations like the National Congress of American Indians, the National Indian Youth Council, and the Alaska Federation of Natives are exerting positive leadership in urban and reservation life. Through litigation, many tribes are seeking economic and political autonomy. They are finding that in solidarity there is strength. Government is becoming more responsive to the people's needs.

The ceremonies and sacraments of the tribal cultures were

[6] Cahn and Hearne, eds., *Our Brother's Keeper*, p. 69.
[7] *Ibid.*, p. 71.

designed to heal the body and renew the spirit. Where they have not survived, there has been little to take their place. A young Navajo woman writes: "The Indian spirit has been the last hope of mankind. Make it breathe by walking in the old ways."[8]

Today, as in the past, Indian women are acting out the tribal ethic of cooperation and service to the community. They are entering every field, from politics to the arts, and blending the spiritual values of the old world with competencies gained in the new. They are, in the words of poet Lois Jircitano, "not a sacred relic but a legacy of strength."[9]

[8] Lorrena Deal, abridged from a letter in *The Navajo Times,* Albuquerque, New Mexico (January–May 1973).

[9] Lois Bissell Jircitano, "Love, Grandma," *Akwesasne Notes,* Rooseveltown, New York (Summer 1975), p. 3.

1.

I KEEP WONDERING HOW I WILL SURVIVE IN THIS STRANGE ENVIRONMENT

I SEE STRANGE FACES AROUND ME

BELLE JEAN FRANCIS ATHABASCAN

A young woman who arrived in Chicago in 1968 describes the shock of being separated from the extended family of the reservation and thrust into the impersonal environment of the big city.

Here I am in a big city, right in the middle of Chicago. I don't know anybody. I am so lonesome and I have that urge to go home. I don't know which direction to go—south, north, east, or west. I can't just take any direction because I don't know my way around yet.

I see strange faces around me and I keep wondering how I will survive in this strange environment. I keep wondering how I can get over this loneliness, and start adjusting to this environment. I know I have to start somewhere along the line and get involved in social activities and overcome the fear I am holding inside me and replace it with courage, dignity, self-confidence, and the ambition to reach my goal.

Before I can adjust myself to this strange environment and get involved in things, I need friends who will help me overcome this urge to go home so I can accomplish my goal here in this unknown world which I entered.

THE TWENTIETH-CENTURY ATROCITY
LAURA WATERMAN WITTSTOCK SENECA

Ms. Wittstock is a journalist. She was born on the Cattaraugus Indian Reservation in western New York and is a member of the Heron clan of the Hodenosaunee, The Longhouse People.

After World War II, there was a move to relocate Indians, to get them off reservations, supposedly as a solution to their economic problems. Actually, it was a way of reducing federal responsibility for education and social services to Indians. Many of our people felt themselves abandoned.

This is still going on. Government and industry are still violating treaties and appropriating tribal lands, leaving the people without any means of support.

Government programs to help Indian people adapt to a new life in the cities have been inadequate. The people are separated from their tribe, from an atmosphere which gave them security. Yet they're not integrated into the larger society; nor do they want to be. What they do want is recognition of their cultural integrity. And they want the financial assistance to develop the educational, cultural, and job-training programs that will restore their pride and self-sufficiency.

The government's neglect of the urban Indian is absurd. It's the twentieth-century atrocity!

Laura Wittstock. Photograph by Roger L. Woo.

IN THE SHALLOWS
BARBARA WOLF BOOTH SIOUX

For those who have lost the security of the old world and have not found a place in the new there is the sense of being in limbo, of going nowhere.

I have had tomorrow
stripped from
My soul,
When all seemed
Certain.
The future
No longer clutters
my mind,
Because there is
None.
Buried like
A dog's old bone
Discarded
To be dug
At leisure
At their convenience,
You didn't fit
The scheme
Of things
The shallows have overtaken the
dreams.

AUGUST 24, 1963–1:00 A.M.: OMAHA
DONNA WHITEWING SIOUX-WINNEBAGO

The daughter of a migrant farm worker, Ms. Whitewing was born in Nebraska in 1943. She attended the Institute for American Indian Arts in Santa Fe, New Mexico.

Heavy breathing fills all my chamber
Sinister trucks prowl
    down dim-lit alleyways.
Racing past each other,
    cars toot obscenities.
Silence is crawling in open windows
    smiling and warm.
Suddenly,
    crickets and cockroaches
    join in the madness:
    cricking and crawling.
Here I am!
A portion of some murky design.
Writing,
    because I cannot sleep,
    because I could die here.

MY GRANDMOTHER TALKED TO THE WATER
MARY MCDANIEL CHEYENNE RIVER SIOUX

A great-granddaughter of the Sioux chief Gall, Mary McDaniel barely subsists on a meager income from the beaded moccasins and jewelry she makes by hand. In her kitchenless room in Oakland, California, this grandmother of twelve recalls a time when "we never went hungry."

After I was born, we went up to Cheyenne River. I'm enrolled there. My number is 3,872 . . . I have some land up there—I don't know how many acres. I get $17 a year for it. There's buffalo grass on it, but alkali water; the water is no good. When my grandmother died, they took her land to pay back her old-age assistance she had been paid. They held the lease checks for fourteen years to pay that back. The BIA does that. . . .

When I was a little girl at Cheyenne River, my grandmother used to part my hair in the middle and color the part yellow and put on a white plume so I wouldn't be struck by lightning. We used to have to go down to the creek every morning. My grandmother talked to the water. Before we washed, she would tell it how beautiful it was and thank it for cleansing her. She used to tell me to listen to the water, and then she would sing a song to it. You know the sound water makes? When she sang, it sounded just like the water.

One day we were with my grandmother and there were coyotes whining. She went out and fed them because that's what Great Spirit said to do, to take care of the herd.

You know I used to play in the fields and eat those little yellow flowers.

We lived in a big log house. But we used a tipi in the summertime to be cool. When you feel sick, you hear the wind in the top of the tipi and it makes you well again. I used to help with the work, carry water, and cook. But when an Indian woman's part of the month comes around, she can't touch food and she's supposed to stay out of the tent.

We kept ourselves clean; I don't know why they call us dirty Indians . . . We used to use oil and an herb for scent, and mud to make our skin smooth.

We had a lot of things like that. To learn what herbs to use, you followed a wounded animal to see what he eats. And when my grandmother pulled a medicine root out of the ground, she used to shove tobacco in the hole to pay back Great Spirit . . . We used to use a leaf, like marijuana, too, and smoke the animals with it to calm them, but only the medicine man could use it. The secrets died with them, because they knew the white man would brainwash us. We had birth control too; you could drink the tea of a tall weed and you wouldn't have children.

In the 1930s, we moved back to Pine Ridge. You should have seen the people when they first got their commodities; they threw all the flour away, they didn't know what to do with it. But we never went hungry. My mother's father, Joe Wounded Horse, was chief of police and a scout during the Indian Wars, and my father was an agriculturist. There was a picture of our log house in the BIA office, and a sign under it that said, "The house that corn built." My father worked all summer, and when he harvested, they all came and he gave away whatever he didn't need. He used to kill elk too, and pass it out to old-age people. He used to say, "This is what you used to eat, and I know you're still hungry for it." They voted him to be chairman of the Pine Ridge Council, but he was a Canadian Sioux, so he couldn't hold office. He was a Republican. He said anybody can be a Democrat, but to be a Republican you have to keep your feet on the ground and never cheat. I'm a Republican too.

I went to boarding school. You were punished there if you talked Indian. After you got used to it, it wasn't bad.

They called us full bloods "blues" at the boarding school, because we were so dark. The mixed-bloods were real light. They used to point at us in the shower, and the matron punished us more than she punished the mixed-bloods. I was proud to be a full blood, but in my own mind. I didn't express it out loud, because it was no use.

Our English teacher called us idiots. But I always studied my spelling. If I missed a word, I'd write that word a hundred times. Now I do crossword puzzles. That's why I buy the paper. I learned it from my father. . . .

I finished the eleventh grade before I ran off and got married. My father wouldn't give me twenty dollars, so the next Friday night I eloped, and got married on their wedding day. I married Daniel McMasters—he was part Mexican. . . .

I wasn't in love with Daniel McMasters. My mother told me, "When you're in love, it's always like you're at a lake with nice cool water and green trees." It wasn't like that with Daniel McMasters. I regretted it from the day it started. It must have been infatuation, because it sure wore off fast. But I stuck it out for four years until my father died, because my father didn't believe in divorce. I had two children.

After I got divorced, I moved to Custer, and never went back to the reservation no more. At Custer I worked in civil service in the factory there, cuttin' mica for the airplanes. I met my second husband there. He was working at the planing factory, finishing lumber. He was French and Russian.

We moved to Oakland in 1954, and he started drinking. We used to sing and play guitar in the bars. My husband played rhythm and I played the chords, and we sang Western. We made money, enough to keep up our bills. . . .

We got divorced in 1958. He beat me up and broke my jaw so I couldn't eat, and I had tuberculosis. The judge put my children in a foster home until I got well.

I got married again in 1960. He passed away in 1965. I had three husbands; when I get to heaven, I won't be lonely. . . .

I don't owe nobody now, but I have my rent, eighteen dollars a week.[1] I'm so worried, I don't know what to do. When you're here, you're like in a rat race, wondering what's going to happen. There on the reservation people are happy to see you. Here the people are happy to see you too, but you wonder what they want. Our word for the white man is *was'ichu,* the one who takes everything, the greedy one. I don't know what to do about my rent; that place is no good anyway. I have some beadwork out, but they haven't paid me. I sew for people too. It takes about a day and a half to make a headband. I make medallions too, with the peace sign, or your initials. I made a lot of those medallions with matching earrings. The medallions sold, but the earrings didn't do too well. It takes a long time to do that work. First, you got to

[1] This interview was first published in 1971.—J. K.

pick your beads, and right now, beads are hard to get. I think it must be the Russians in Czechoslovakia; they make the best beads there. You get the clay beads and get them wet, they melt. The glass beads, the water washes the color right off. Now I have mostly black and white beads and a little drawer of red and yellow, but I need blue.

A HOLDING BATTLE AGAINST DISEASE
BELVA COTTIER ROSEBUD SIOUX

In January 1976, twelve persons, some of them Indians, perished in a San Francisco Bay Area apartment-house fire. The newspaper Wassaja *cited overcrowding and unsafe conditions as reasons for the fire. The building had been condemned by the fire department two years before, but its owners had managed to evade prosecution. Ms. Belva Cottier, Director of the Native American Health Clinic, recently funded to serve 45,000 Indian people in the area, was shocked by the insensitivity of public officials who permit such dangerous conditions to exist.*

Housing is the root of the evils we must contend with. Unless this is remedied, we are merely fighting a holding battle against disease, malnutrition, alcoholism, and desperately unsafe conditions.

I sometimes wonder what's the use of treating a sick child and then sending him back to the hovel where his illness started in the first place.

I DON'T LIKE BIG TOWNS
BAFFIN ISLAND ESKIMO

In just a generation, Eskimo life-styles have changed rapidly. Many have left behind the hunting and fishing culture of their ancestors and have moved to cities in search of jobs. Frobisher Bay is a growing community on Baffin Island in Canada's Northwest Territories. The influx of Eskimos from small outlying settlements has led to a severe housing shortage. Large families crowd into tiny cubicles, often substandard and condemned, creating severe health and fire hazards. Unemployment is widespread. One local resident gives her view of the situation.

My biggest complaint is about the housing and the land—the way they're changing. I grow up in a small community. There was good land, good weather, and good people. Healthy. I didn't know anything about any alcohol.

When I moved to Frobisher Bay I didn't like it. The people are different. I got used to it; then it was fine. Since I married in 1962 we live in an apartment. I have three kids. We have four or five neighbors wall-to-wall. When my kids start running, we just don't fit into the place.

I would like to live in the north. Most of the hunters like to live close to the water. But the government put all their small houses far from the water.

Hudson Bay used to have lovely houses close to the shore. Every summer my Mom always liked to set her tent close to the shore so she could clean her fish and other things from the salty water.

We don't have any dog team or skidoo, no taxi. Every summer the Eskimo hunters have to drag their seals and fish way up to their houses. It's difficult for them.

Before the government set the houses up they should have asked the people who lived in the community. We're still alive. We're not slaves yet.

So much gravel and dirt has been moved from the land. It's not attractive. And I don't know where the money goes. I don't like big towns. When Eskimo people move to them from small settlements they can't find jobs. I don't like to see so many people not doing anything, and not helping each other.

WE WILL SURVIVE

JANET MCCLOUD DUWAMISH

This mother of eight is active in the Northwest tribes' legal battle for fishing rights. She joined the movement when her husband, who was unable to make a living as a fisherman, was forced to go to work for an electric company to support the family.

They put Indians into city ghettos and make industrial slaves of them. . . . If the spirit grows within us, we'll survive. We will survive . . .

2.

RETURN TO THE HOME WE MADE

ON THE RESERVATION, THE OLD PEOPLE WATCH THE CARS GO BY RITA DILLE OJIBWE (CHIPPEWA)

Most reservation communities tend to be rural, and fairly isolated. Conservative attitudes persist. Many of the young people attend school in nearby cities or migrate to large urban areas in search of better schools, jobs, and wider social experience. Those who return or visit the reservation often sense the gap between old ways and new. Rita Dille was fourteen and a student in an urban school when she wrote of visits to her grandparents' reservation home.

On the reservation the old people walk to town or just sit at home and watch the cars go by. In the log shack the old women sit and bead headbands or something. They cook rabbit soup, boiled potatoes, and wild rice. In the evening the old men and women sit around and talk about things that happened when they were young or tell each other Indian stories. In the wintertime my grandpa goes and chops ice for water. Us girls hide so when our grandpa goes we can follow him to the lake and slide on ice. After a while we go into the house and help him cook.

All there is in town is the Tomahawk Bar, The Red Owl, the hotel, the café, and the gas station, and that's it!

Sioux woman. Photograph by Leslie Bush.

WE LIVED ON THE RIVER
LOUISE HIETT CHEYENNE RIVER SIOUX

Ms. Hiett was interviewed in 1971 at her home in Eagle Butte, South Dakota, as part of the University of South Dakota's Oral History project. Then eighty-four years old, she looked back on her early years on the reservation.

My father was a rancher. I was seventeen years old when I finished eighth grade. That was as far as the government was teaching Indian children in them days . . . We just stayed home and helped our parents. I did. I rode horseback. I took care of the cattle, took care of the milk cows and the horses. When it was branding time, why I was right in the midst of it. I mowed hay; I raked hay; I hauled hay. We had to put up hay in the summer to feed our cattle in the winter. Well, it was the same routine every year and we got along fine . . .

Oh, the country was beautiful and I remember this, beautiful grass all over. We lived on the river and it was all grass. In the summertime, my Dad built a little log-house ranch up on the foot of the hills. We bring our cattle there and we summer our cattle up here with lots of lake beds—water, you know. And the grass was so thick, why we herded our cattle up here away from the river bottom. And the Indian boys worked . . . And I was just a young girl, but I'd go and cook for them boys.

I ALWAYS FELT TRULY INDIAN
GERTRUDE BUCKANAGA OJIBWE (CHIPPEWA)

Originally from the White Earth Reservation in northern Minnesota, Ms. Buckanaga now lives in Minneapolis. She is on the faculty of St. Catherine's College in St. Paul where she counsels Native American students. She says: "Many of our graduates are returning to their native communities. I'll be back up north some day too."

I spent my early years on the Ojibwe Reservation in Pine Point, Minnesota. We had a large family, with seven children. We were very close. I always felt truly Indian. My mother used to say: "Wherever you go, whatever you do, hold your head up and be proud you're Indian."

One of the first homes that I remember was a log house with one big room. We didn't have electricity, TV, or even a radio. Then we moved into a government rehabilitation home. It was small too, but the rooms were divided. We used an oil lamp, and a wood-burning stove. We still had no electricity and no indoor plumbing.

Those were the Depression years, and we were poor. We all had to work. We cut wood for fuel. We set traps for rabbits which the family ate. There were no baby-sitters in those days. Today, if a child is left alone with older children, the Welfare will come in and say that the child is neglected. But within Indian families, it was accepted that the older children would care for the younger ones. Children of six or seven—boys as well as girls—learned to change diapers. We always knew what was expected of us. This is typical of Indian families. We learned to cooperate and share.

We had a garden every year. All the children from age four or five worked in it. We were taught how to pull weeds, how to use the hoe. Each of us had a task. During the fall of the year, our family went ricing. We camped near the rice beds where we met other Indian families. It was a good experience . . .

Now I have four children of my own, and I want to pass the old values on to them. The respect for older people, the sharing, the caring for each other, I'd like to see us hang on to that.

NEWS FROM OLD CROW
EDITH JOSIE LOUCHEUX

Edith Josie is from Old Crow, a town 120 miles south of the Arctic Ocean in Canada's Yukon Territory. She writes the news for a periodical, The Whitehorse Star. *Her bulletins have appeared in* Life *and on CBC.*

January 3
Women dog race held today. Nine teams was in the race. Sorry, the time sheet is lost. It was tack up on the post and the kids have torn it off. Only four times remember is first two teams and middle two teams.

Mrs. Clara Tizyah took first place with the time of eight min. thirteen sec. Clara is using Paul Ben Kassi team and look as though Clara made better time than Paul so must be Clara is better musher than Paul.

January 21
Since Jan. 20 it start to be sunshine and sure look beautiful. No caribou and lots of them got no meat and no grub and lots of them are hungry. When it's nothing to eat and it's sure bad for big family. Mr. Chief Charlie Peter he sure had big family and he had about ten kids and himself and his wife. They were twelve in his house. They really got nothing no meat.

May 18
I went to Mr. Netro store and I ask him how much rat skin he get and he told me how much he get.

Since February March April and May he got about 20,447 rat skins from the boys in Old Crow. If rat house is good they would killed more but not very good. Cause some rat house is frozen and what is good to set trap for caribou eat the rat house and spoil it.

The caribou is bad for eating rat house when there are no grass and they have to eat rat house. This is why it is hard to get rat this spring. So some boys will go to work at camp. I hope they don't get fire and work steady.

July 28

I been to Inuvik and sure lots of car. Old Crow no car also no airport and phone. These three should be in Old Crow. If these thing in our small town be big surprise for people. Not much fish here this summer.

September 28

Mr. Peter Moses has been doing lots of work when he alive on this earth. He was happy old man and friendly with anybody even with the white people. So I know everybody will miss him but hope he will have a good rest. He was very kind to the kids most and all the kids like him. When he sees the boys and girls, he talk silly and laugh. When someone make feast he make speech everyone like because he make everyone laugh.

And when the dance is on, he always make jig with his wife. He always make double jig with the girls. He was born on the American side and the year he was born is 1882. I hear he married in 1901. On September 28, he came back from upriver because he spit blood but he was very good and he's not sick. So no one know he was going to die. While that he pass away sure everybody surprise for him. . . .

All the men make coffin for him and they going to dig ground for him on Oct. 2.

They will have funeral service on Oct. 3. Everybody will go to service and the graveyard. That much we miss him. Some women make a beautiful flowers for his graveyard. They will have English and Indian hymn and prayer. Even the school kids will go to service so will have English hymn for him. If the weather is clear some people will fly in to the funeral. . . .

October 10
They see caribous on mountain and the snow is on mountain. Sure look like winter.

Those carpenter and the electric are sure busy every day.

They just call Old Crow town and they should say Old Crow is town now because everyone had lights and lights is on the street and sure look different as before. Soon it get dark the lights is on. Sure look very good.

IN THE NIGHT SKY
MARY PITSEOLAK ESKIMO

The stonecut on the next page was done in 1961 by Mary Pitseolak, an artist from the Cape Dorset artists' community on Baffin Island in the Canadian Eastern Arctic.

In the Night Sky. Stonecut by Mary Pitseolak.

RETURN TO THE HOME WE MADE
DOLLY BIRD

Born in Minnesota in 1950, Dolly Bird has lived most recently in New York. She reacts to the anonymity of life in the city, and recalls her home on the plains where "the Gods watched us."

Hey my man
you know we can't
stay in these city trappings
You know it my man
so hey
we been squatting too long
on land that ain't never
gonna be ours

There's no jobs
and the want ads
offer equal opportunities
done filled this morning
Hey we're good
don't need this crud

From where we're at
we can see
a travel agency and
I don't guess I'm
for Miami this season
but oh hey let us
go Rocky Mountain delving

Remember where we used to live
when John Wayne never came around
and Gunsmoke came out

of your rifle
let's hock next year
for this instant
and when we sell out
next January
at least we will have spent
some good times

We have been null and void
a sight too long
I'm thinking we could
go home

And if we don't make it
we'd a done something

I've seen you remember
'cause I've seen you cry
Crying with dry eyes
and your blood bursting
at the thought
of untrod plains,
the beaver woods
and I've seen your eyes travel south
over the memorized outlines
of sun silhouetted buttes
down into a wash
before the August rains
when we spoke
a beautiful language
and the Gods watched us
We could see them too
as we huddled in a cave
of a canyon in a desert storm
when thunder rolled and
crashed against red orange

purple echo walls
and then a rainbow grew
where lightning was planted
Yes I know you cried
'cause I was crying too

I know you're aching
to ride the Appaloosa
who knew your destination
by the mood of your kick
I did love to see
you all over leather
in the distance
and to feel
the trembling ground
as you rode closer
and nights with
a separate dusk and evening
when after fry bread
and fresh venison
we leaned our shoulders
into the rising heat
of our sacred fire

Oh strong man
please, we can't go on
remembering only
the home we made
out of what we found
and a warm quilt's sleep
We must go back
We're talking sounds
that we don't understand
We're down but please
We could try

They've mock laughed at us
We awkward tripping from
the street to where people walk
the skin-burst clay
Our confused eyes
unable to focus
on all them at once moving
Your years molded muscles
are outmoded here
City people putting us down
as ignorant because
our knowledge is wisdom
not a library
and we ain't needed
here

Now, it must be now
our round trip
Complete the circle
while we can see
a flat-eared cougar
and can you tell
how many days passed
after these tracks of wolves
and which way is
the big snow blowing
and which is the root
to calm the fever

Now you lift your heart
with something stirring
starting to rustle in you
Asking me if we've
got enough salt 'n lard
and is dog sleeping
outside the door
and maybe we could

somehow get
a few sheep of our own
or cattle seeing as now
they're no trouble at all

THERE IS NO WORD FOR *GERM* IN OUR LANGUAGE
ANNIE DODGE WAUNEKA NAVAJO

Indian health care on reservations is inadequate. Public health facilities are understaffed and often remote from centers of Indian population. Lacking transportation, Indians often don't make it to the hospital or are dead on arrival. Then too, some still rely on the midwife and the medicine man. The problem is many-faceted, according to Ms. Wauneka, Navajo tribal leader. The Navajo, she says, still views sickness as a sign that he or she is out of harmony with the natural order.

Today, when a Navajo becomes ill, he must choose between the white man's doctor and his own medicine man. He has to decide which one will cure him. In the past, the Navajo people did not believe in the spread of disease, and this is still true today with a majority of them.

There is no word for *germ* in our language. This makes it hard for the Navajo people to understand sickness . . . It is very hard for the Navajo, especially the older ones who have tuberculosis, to go far from home, because they have never been off the reservation or far from their loved ones.

A hospital is totally strange to them—strange people, strange food, strange ways of treating the sick. Bathing facilities, running water, electric lights, and thermometers are all strange . . . All this must be explained.

Such foods as vegetables, fish, chicken, and pork are not part of the regular Navajo diet; so this is something else they must learn. The value of these foods must be explained, as well as the value of the drugs and treatment the doctor recommends.

I WANT TO BE A CHRISTIAN
LAURA ZIEGLER BRULÉ SIOUX

Ms. Ziegler was born in 1890 on the Lower Brulé reservation in South Dakota. She was interviewed there in 1971. She said that she had taught school, and was a member of the Indian Rights Association.

We got these two missionaries [Roman Catholic and Episcopalian], but they not working for the benefit of the Indians . . . There's Reverend Hollum [Assembly of God] . . . he saved a lot of lives. A lot of people would have died before they could have got to the hospital. There he was and he would give first aid and help out. Many times he took his own car. He's a credit to the place. He's faithful . . .

Now they got the C.H.R. [Community Health Representative] in here. There's nights when we want somebody in, there's nobody on duty. It's the same with the police outfit. Sometimes things are going on and we really need a policeman. Now last winter a boy was hurt. He was beat up and cut—he was all bloody. So I went back and told his grandmother. Well, they got Reverend Hollum. He got in there and gave him first aid. Police, they never done anything about it. . . .

I want to be a Christian. I want to be it all the way through because I do my Christian rights. I feed many people. If there's children come and ask me for something to eat, I gave them sometime and went without myself. But I've never broadcasted it or anything, because I don't think when you do something good you should do that. I always figure you get it back in some other ways . . .

WOOL SEASON
PAULA GUNN ALLEN LAGUNA

Ms. Allen is from the Cubero land grant in New Mexico. There, much of the land is denuded of vegetation; crumbling roads are periodically washed out by violent rainstorms. Isolated from markets and faced with competition from synthetic, petroleum-based textiles, the people cannot sell their wool. There is a sense of futility; they are victims of modern technology.

In Cubero
days too hot, arroyo dry
dust marks the road that forever crumbles at the edge
it will rain next month. Now
time to get the wool in—weighed, paid up, settled,
like in the good times when wool sold by the tons,
even out of Cubero.
Now it's petroleum all the way, and the arroyo gets deeper,
the road narrows a little every year.
Old Diego died in the bottom of the arroyo
a couple of years ago. They say he was drunk,
missed his way in the dark. They found him in the morning.
The old huge boulders I climbed have shattered or moved down-
stream
in summer floods. The heavy hum of fat flies is the same.

What do the people do when they can't sell their wool?
How do they settle for the lard and mutton and flour?
The kids clothes, the ladies' shawls, the shovels,
the tires, the gas?
The wool lies heavy in the barn now, season after season,
unsold, unwanted. No one even tans the hides.
They can't survive much more. Being punished for no crimes.
The skin of my thought is bloody wool, stuffed
with gorging ticks like the packed sacks of fleece.

Don't play in the barn where the wool is stacked
they used to warn us kids,
you'll be killed whether you've murdered anyone or not.

OUR CHILDREN KNOW NOTHING ABOUT THEIR HERITAGE
LILA MCCORTNEY NISQUALLY-QUINAULT

When she was interviewed in December 1975, Ms. McCortney was proprietor of Lila's Gift Shop, a small store featuring native crafts on the Quinault Reservation in Clearwater, Washington. A slim, small-boned woman, she appeared much younger than her seventy-six years. During a torrential downpour, she took time from her work to talk about her life.

I'm half-blooded. I was born into the Nisqually tribe. My parents died when I was five, and I was put in an Indian Boarding School in Tacoma. I was there till I was fifteen; then they closed the school, and we were sent out to learn a trade. I became a housekeeper for my aunt in Tacoma. When I was nineteen, I married a member of the Quinault tribe and was adopted into the tribe. After my husband died, I went into ranching and raising beef cattle—there's not much money in it—and settled here. My boy built this shop for me out of a garage.

I started this little shop so the people in the village would have a place to sell their handicrafts. But they tripled their prices on me, and now I sell very little. Just like any place, I've gone commercial. I have things here you can buy anywhere; I have to make a living. The villagers bring me their work. I pay them and add one or two dollars for myself when I sell them. I used to have better things. Maggie, down the road, is the best basketmaker in the village. She made that raffia basket. But she's eighty-nine now. Her eyesight is bad—cataracts. She remembers the old times, the legends. Sometimes she sits right in that chair and goes on and on about the old times.

See this basket? It's bear grass. The smaller ones are always more expensive because they're harder to make. There is only one strip on the reservation where bear grass grows now. You have to know how to cut the bear grass—you grab it in clumps down at the roots. But with all the logging that's going on here they cut the trees down, and there is no shade for the bear grass to grow. The grass is green; it's cured and then dyed. We never made our own dyes here; they use commercial dyes. Those old baskets are not for sale.

The Indians are doing beadwork now, made of glass. These shell necklaces are made by our children here in the village. They find the shells on the beach. And these headbands—the hippies went crazy for them and bought almost all of them a few years ago. That wood carving of a wild deer being attacked was made by a boy here in the village. He was nine when he made it. He is eleven now. He wants $50 for it. They make their own prices.

Our children know nothing of their culture and heritage. In the old days we made baskets and we traded them for food and other necessities. Now there are so few basketmakers left—it's a lost art. The youngsters are not interested in it. They don't want to do the hard work—to pick the grass and dye it. The kids don't seem to care. They do beadwork. It's easier.

Last spring I had lovely baskets. A lady paid $35 without hesitating. But the people only make them in the winter; in the summer they like to travel more. In the winter they stay home; the rains are so bad, and the frost. We've had rain for three months, and everything is flooded.

I'm seventy-six years old. I keep active. I can drive a tractor, but I never could drive a car. I'm a rancher. I walk three miles every day. My barn is near the water. When you came, I was just rounding up some bulls that had wandered off in the rain. I've always done a lot of walking. When I raised my family, I walked on the beach. I know this sounds silly, but I used to walk the beach while I was pregnant. I always had my babies at night, never had a doctor. People said I was crazy. But today they have natural childbirth just like then.

I had five children—now only three are left. My oldest boy, the one who built this shop, was a timber surveyor. He was killed in a car accident. He bought the black walnut panels somewhere and put them up. My oldest girl was fifteen when she died—leakage of the heart. Now they have so many medicines and operations to cure it. Then there was nothing.

One of my daughters gave me this rug. She's married now. She comes often to see me. She rearranges everything in the shop and on the shelves and then when she leaves, I rearrange it all back again. My children gave me the glass windows. The counters are nice. The small one is very old. A few weeks ago a family came in with three boys. They made so much noise and touched everything—one boy sat on the glass counter and smashed it. That's why there's no glass in it. No, they didn't offer to pay anything or say anything to the children, just: "Come on, let's get out of here."

3.

I WISH I COULD LEARN TO TALK INDIAN

IF THE CHILDREN DON'T GET ON . . .

LILA MCCORTNEY NISQUALLY-QUINAULT

With her income as a shopkeeper and rancher on the Quinault Reservation, Ms. McCortney was able to send her children to college.

In this little village, there are about one hundred children, many from different tribes. Many of the people intermarry, or marry whites, so a lot of the children are mixed-bloods.

We have Head Start right here in the village. Six miles up is the grade school. The children are bused to school in Lake Quinault. Then, through the government many of them get grants to go on to college. I have a granddaughter in college in Port Angeles. She's taking up forestry.

I think that if the children don't get on it's their own fault, because they can go on to college if they want to—the federal government pays the tuition. People always say an Indian don't have a chance, but it's really neglect on their part if they don't get an education. When my children went to college, there was no government help. We had to pay for everything.

OL' UNCLE SAM, HE WAS PRETTY GOOD TO US
HENRIETTA CHIEF WINNEBAGO

Ms. Chief was seventy-six years old when she was interviewed on the Winnebago reservation in Nebraska in 1970.

I must have been about eight years old when they took us. My father and mother had parted, and I guess my mom couldn't take care of us all. And there were three of us, and the government, you know, they come and they took us to the Tomah Indian School [Wisconsin]. And that's where we were raised. I was there for about nine years. And about thirteen, fourteen, . . . I don't know which it was, how old I was then—and that's when I was first converted. The superintendent showed slides—that was before moving pictures—he showed slides, and he showed Jesus on the cross with His arms outstretched, you know, like that. Right then and there I accepted Jesus as my Lord and Saviour. That's been over sixty years. And I'm happy, just as I was when I was converted. . . .

I just went as far as eighth grade. Just studied arithmetic and English, and read, you know, and we used to write home letters. My mother and my father used to write us. . . . Oh, I just loved that school, because that's where I was converted. And he was just like a minister, our superintendent. I heard he passed away. Mr. Compton; Allen Compton his name was. And I have no regrets. I had three square meals a day. The government helped me there again. They helped all the time, and they had cattle there . . . they had a herd of cattle there and they had all the milk we wanted and chickens—they raised chickens. And I just went as far as the eighth grade and we came down here . . .

I must have been raised real good, because I remember we ate oatmeal—oatmeal every morning—and eggs, we had eggs. . . . We played games, and I remember one time, the Fourth of July, they used to have fireworks there. . . . We used to have, at the agency you know; and the hospital used to be out there—the government hospital. Had the government hospital, and yeah, ol' Uncle Sam, he was pretty good to us. Some kicked, but I don't.

I AM A METIS
YVONNE MONKMAN METIS

Canada's Metis,[1] descendants of French settlers who intermarried with Indians, suffer the special stigma reserved for those of mixed racial heritage. They are not fully accepted by either the white or Indian communities, and have long been denied political and social equality by Canadian society. Yvonne Monkman teaches in a nursery and kindergarten program in Winnipeg, Manitoba. She is originally from Manigotagan, on the shores of Lake Winnipeg.

When I was a child, there was no recognition in our schools, no mention of my Indian heritage. It was something almost hidden. As I grew older, I began to wonder about my history, and question people about my background. Gradually, I developed a strong sense of who I am.

Most of the children I teach are Metis, and they are confused about their identity. I help them to discover who they are. We Indians teach children to be independent, to make choices at an early age. That's part of the heritage.

I want the children to know what it means to be Indian today. They will have to learn to live in a society that doesn't fully accept them.

This society has to change. People have to learn to question their images and attitudes and to judge each of us as individuals. Only then will doors be open for Indian people.

[1] *Metis:* people of mixed blood.

EVERYBODY ALWAYS DID OUR THINKING FOR US
WINIFRED JOURDAIN OJIBWE (CHIPPEWA)

Ms. Jourdain has served on the board of Upward Bound, a program that offers tutorial services to minority youngsters. At her home in Minneapolis, surrounded by the beaded medallions, moccasins, and ceremonial bags she makes, she talked about education. "I'd like to see young people have the opportunities I never had."

I was born on the White Earth Reservation in Minnesota. My family is Ojibwe. We're God-fearing people.

I went to Bureau of Indian Affairs boarding schools—one of these was on the reservation. If it wasn't for those schools, I don't know where I'd be today. They were the motivating factor in my life. But they tried to make us white, to give us the white culture, to integrate us. We were never allowed to talk our own language. Very few of the children today speak Ojibwe . . .

The biggest enemy the Indian ever had is lack of education. I've helped set up enrichment programs for Indian students in the public schools. But our children don't get the support they need in the home. Our people seem to be very discouraged. They've been denied so much for so long. Just pushed aside, not listened to, all their lives. Everybody always did our thinking for us.

So many Indian children have been turned off by the public schools. There's too little supervision. They get away with too much. Many can't read, can't do math. And many of the teachers just don't expect an Indian child to succeed. The children take advantage of the system, and eventually they drop out. It's been estimated that sixty-eight to seventy percent of our children do not finish school.

If I could take each child by the hand and lead him or her to school, I would.

Ojibwe woman and child. Photograph by Charles Brill, 1971.

IF I HAD A CHANCE?
LOUISE HIETT CHEYENNE RIVER SIOUX

Well, I tell you, I'm eighty-four years old. I went to a government mission school. All we learned was up to the eighth grade. That's as far as the government was teaching Indians children them days . . .

I'm old and I sit here and I think, what if I had a chance? I know I would make use of it.

AH, I KNEW EVERYBODY
SYLVIA WHIPPLE NAVAJO

At the time of her interview in 1972, Ms. Whipple was a student at the University of South Dakota in Vermillion. Her husband was a doctoral candidate.

Here [in South Dakota] I think they don't have the old way; maybe the older people do, but not the ones from my generation. They're in between the old culture and the non-Indian world. They're split . . . Their land was taken away and it's just a checkerboard. You have a white neighbor that doesn't like you; you go to the store and your neighbor doesn't like you.

Back home in Arizona I lived with my grandfather and my mother and my father, and we all spoke Indian, and we lived in a hogan and all my relatives came. We knew who our uncles were and our aunts and my dad's family—and, ah, I knew everybody. My uncle did things for me and, you know, when I was feeling bad, he talked to me; and my aunt, if I wanted to talk to somebody. And if I didn't want to do any work, I'd run to my grandmother.

I don't remember hearing my relatives fighting or having bad feelings toward each other. People think awful things about other people. I can't seem to do that.

FEEL THE COMING RAINS
MELANIE ELLIS ONEIDA

Born in 1957 on the Oneida Reservation in Wisconsin, Ms. Ellis began writing a book of poetry, Joy Rides an Appaloosa, at the age of seventeen. She is a graduate of The Institute of American Indian Arts in Santa Fe, New Mexico.

Feel the coming rains and
speak in Thunder Tongue. If
you do not know these simple
things, then how well do you
know the eagle?

EDUCATION IS EVERYTHING YOU EXPERIENCE
LAURA WATERMAN WITTSTOCK SENECA

Ms. Wittstock, mother of five, is Associate Director of The Red School House in St. Paul, Minnesota, where her youngest child is a student.

There are close to twenty survival schools for Indian children in this country. They're taking a constructive approach—giving the children a positive self-concept and a sense of community. These children will be our leaders someday.

The schools are highly experimental. They're not intimidated by the latest curriculum ideas and methodology. They take the view that education is a totally environmental thing. It's everything you experience in a day—including your home life, the wino you see on the street, the drum that you play, and the songs you sing—that's education.

And that goes back to a very ancient idea of education as it existed within the tribal structure a long time ago. I think that's exciting because you have a strengthening of tribal continuity.

The schools are small enough to give the children an intimate experience. The little children are learning to read. They're moving forward in basic skills. These schools are doing something about education, and they're succeeding.

WHO WAS REALLY THE SAVAGE?
ROSE MARY (SHINGOBE) BARSTOW OJIBWE (CHIPPEWA)

A former member of Minnesota's Indian Affairs Commission, Ms. Barstow is now an Ojibwe Teaching Specialist at the University of

Minnesota. Long involved in the preparation of curriculum materials for schoolchildren, she is currently working on an Ojibwe dictionary. She has thirty-six grandchildren.

I was born at four o'clock in the morning at ricing time in Onamia, Minnesota. The year was 1915. My mother was a converted Catholic. She didn't abide by all the traditional rites that were a part of the life pattern of Ojibwe families, so I didn't go through a naming ceremony. When I was two or three, an old lady felt sorry for me and gave me her name, Majigikwewis, and a feast. . . .

I was seven when my mother died. She had been in the hospital for a long time. My grandmother and grandfather raised me. When I turned eight, I went away to a Catholic mission boarding school. My mother had requested that I be sent there. Such a request was always honored by the old people. It was the first time in my life that I was left alone with absolute strangers.

The sisters at the school wore black and I was afraid of them. One of the first things they did was cut my braids off. They made me wear a gingham dress with a big bow. I looked like everybody else. I felt really lost.

They put me in a kindergarten class because I could speak only Ojibwe. I was willing to learn English. One of the girls was asked to read out loud in English. She made a mistake, and the whole class began to laugh. I had been brought up not to laugh at a person who made a mistake—if he made it over and over you felt sorry for him. I thought those children were crude. Even the teacher had a glint in her eye. So I zipped up my mouth, and made up my mind that nobody was going to laugh at me for trying.

I was dumb all that year; never spoke a word. But I was learning internally. I worked so hard at learning English, I almost forgot my Ojibwe. When I returned home in the summer, I could hardly talk to Grandma and Grandfather. I was embarrassed. My aunt didn't understand what was wrong with me. She accused me of having foolish pride in myself—*bishigwadis*—that's a terrible insult to our people, because we're taught that you're never an entity by yourself. You're always a part of something. So I made up my mind to show her, to relearn Ojibwe so I could converse properly with my grandparents. By the end of the summer I was fluent in the language.

Our summers were happy. On Sundays, Grandfather would catch the horse, we'd jump in the buggy and go to church in the town where our relatives lived. One Sunday it was Episcopal, the next Methodist. We sat in the back row and learned to respect other religions. We learned that what's important is not what religion you practice, but believing in what you've been taught. Others will respect you for it.

I went back to school in the fall. Now that I could speak English, I never kept my mouth shut. We read a history book about "the savages." The pictures were in color. There was one of a group of warriors attacking white people—a woman held a baby in her arms. I saw hatchets, blood dripping, feathers flying. I showed the picture to the Sister. She said, "Rose Mary, don't you know you're Indian?" I said, "No, I'm not." She said, "Yes, you are." I said, "No!" And I ran behind a clump of juniper trees, and cried and cried. I spent a week in the infirmary. I didn't eat. I was really sick.

When I went home I told Grandfather. He said, "I've heard about those books. They call us savages. Some of our old people wonder who was really the savage. Whites came here with a man nailed to a cross and used it to subdue us. They took everything from us. They said that we scalped our enemies. But you know, they bought Indian scalps for a dollar a head. That's not in those history books. You must return to school, Rose Mary. The Great Spirit gave you a mind of your own. Someday, my girl, you will write the truth in our language. You will write of the goodness of our people, and the tranquility."

I WISH I COULD LEARN TO TALK INDIAN
LINDA MARTINEAU OJIBWE (CHIPPEWA)

Tribal people have always equated age with wisdom. Yet the young people's unfamiliarity with the traditional languages has resulted in an ever-widening gap between old and young. Linda Martineau was fifteen and a student in a public junior high school when she expressed this concern.

My grandma Katy is just a tiny thing. I used to stay with her when she lived alone. I liked to help her in every way. I could cook, clean, and anything else I could do. But now she's too old to stay alone so she stays with her daughter.

I like to sit and talk to her but it seems to me her mind went back for many years. Sometimes she's funny. She talks to me in Indian, and I can't understand most of the stuff she says. That's why I wish I could learn to talk Indian. But then maybe it will be too late for me to sit and talk to her.

4.

A LEGACY OF STRENGTH

PARENTS ARE FOR LOVING
LADONNA HARRIS COMANCHE

Ms. Harris fulfills many roles—as the mother of three and the wife of former United States Senator Fred Harris, and as a dynamic leader in national organizations working to end poverty and discrimination against tribal people. The granddaughter of a Peyote medicine man, she was raised in the secure atmosphere of her grandparents' farm home and didn't become aware of her people's deprivation until she reached adolescence.

I didn't grow up resisting being an Indian the way, unfortunately, so many others do. I was as proud as my grandparents were to be Indian, and the only thing I was sensitive about as a child was that I had light hair and blue eyes.[1] All the rest of the family was dark-haired and dark-eyed.

We children were never physically punished. What kept us in line was the importance of winning the approval and praise of the family, because if we did something silly, the teasing and joking could be unbearable.

If we were really out of line, we were simply ignored, and that was worse than any other type of punishment. If any other discipline was needed, one of our aunts or older cousins was called in, because in the Indian way, parents are more for loving than scolding or punishing.

[1] Her Comanche mother had married an Irishman; they separated shortly after LaDonna's birth.

Young Woman. Stonecut by Shekoalook, 1959.

INDIAN WOMEN HAVE ALWAYS BEEN STRONG
GERTRUDE BUCKANAGA OJIBWE (CHIPPEWA)

As I was growing up, I didn't feel overburdened with household chores. Tasks were shared equally by boys and girls. We learned to work together and to respect each other. I was never made to feel that my place was in the home.

I was free to choose, develop my interests.

Today, I'm accepted as an equal by my husband. That's a good feeling. I haven't had to struggle to achieve it.

Indian women have always been strong. They've kept families together.

I AM A LAKOTA WOMAN
BEA MEDICINE HUNKPAPA SIOUX

An anthropologist, Professor Medicine has done extensive research on the changing roles and expectations of tribal women. She feels it is important to look at "research on what happened in the past between the sexes that determined the role-playing in the various cultures now."

I am a Lakota[2] woman, Hunkpapa Band, and I know exactly who I am and how to relate to men, no matter who they are, and I think that's part of being a woman . . .

The term *Indian woman* conceals and distorts the rich variation that we have in our tribal societies. The roles of women are very different; for example, Navajo society is extremely different from Lakota society, and the roles of women are a reflection of the cultural milieu of that society.

[2] *Lakota:* in the Sioux language, a reference to the Western Sioux.

For almost three centuries, we have not had power or socio-economic clout to determine our destinies . . . Many of us are from a hyphenated background because of the years of BIA boarding schools, parochial boarding schools, and the tremendous amount of intermarriage that has occurred among us . . . This poses another problem to us in examining our own roles. That is, simply, how do we see ourselves? In this kind of hyphenated situation, do we see ourselves as Hopi, or Sioux? This has tremendous implications to our identity and our actions and the way we were socialized in a tribal society . . .

We are the primary socializers of our children. Culture is transmitted primarily through the mother. The mother teaches language, attitudes, beliefs, behavioral patterns, etc. . . .

We all have a rich resource at hand and that is the older women on our reservations. Many of us overlook them. We have so much to learn from them. In recent anthropological literature, there are emerging many life histories that deal with . . . the way women have seen their roles and adjusted; for there is one thing that has allowed us to remain Native American and that is the flexibility that we have learned at our mothers' and fathers' knees.

INDIAN MEDICINE HAS SOME VALIDITY

CONSTANCE PINKERMAN, M.D. CHEROKEE-CHOCTAW

California anaesthesiologist Dr. Pinkerman was in private practice for fifteen years, and earned up to $100 an hour for her services. After a near-fatal illness, she reevaluated her life, and gave up the practice: "I didn't really need the bucks." She joined the Association of American Indian Physicians and learned how critical medical conditions are on Indian reservations and in cities with large Indian populations.

Constance Pinkerman, M.D. Photograph courtesy *Minneapolis Tribune*.

I organized the first free medical center for Indians in the Los Angeles area. I became a street doctor in order to care for Indians who lost eligibility for health-care services when they moved to the city.

Indian medicine has some validity. After all, the first U.S. Pharmacopoeia listed four hundred Indian medicines. Indian medicine was further advanced than Western medicine when Europeans came to America. Indians invented the syringe.

A medicine man says prayers. If you believe in him, you can gain strength from his strength. I guess it's a form of psychotherapy.

BEATING THE DRUM FOR OURSELVES
GRACE THORPE SAUK-FOX

Daughter of famed Indian athlete Jim Thorpe, Ms. Thorpe is a large, jovial woman with varied interests. She has sold real estate and has been a coordinator for a university serving Indians and Chicanos. Like her fiery ancestor Chief Black Hawk, she is an activist and has been jailed for her participation in demonstrations staged by tribal people.

I was born in Yale, Oklahoma, the same place my father was, and I went to the same Indian boarding school that he did. My mother was a white woman and when I was still small, my parents got divorced. I spent the first part of my life traveling back and forth between them.

Most of my years have been spent in advertising and public relations. I sold *Yellow Pages* to businesses for twelve years in New York. One day I woke up in the home I had lived in for twelve years and said, "What am I doing here? I should be working for my people." So I sold my house and quit my job . . . Everyone thought I was crazy, but I knew it was the right thing to do.

I left New York and worked for a year for the National Congress of American Indians. My job was to interest industry in building plants on various Indian reservations. There's no reason we can't train our own people. Let Indians train Indians . . .

We Indian women decided to start beating the drum for ourselves. We formed the National Indian Women's Action Corps. We want all Indian women who want to be active to join us in finding solutions to our problems.

Indian children are still sent away from home to attend boarding schools, and the urban families usually have little time to spend together. We want to change this and encourage stronger family units.

THE WOMAN IS THE DOMINANT FIGURE
MARY MOREZ NAVAJO

Since the age of five when she wove a rug following her own original design, Mary Morez has been immersed in art, and her work has been widely exhibited. She works in acrylics, oils, watercolors, and mixed media, and she draws inspiration from Navajo religion, ceremonials, and folk culture. She uses symbolism and stylized Indian forms to convey her vision of the universal condition of humanity. (*See the cover photograph of her.*)

In Navajo society, the woman is the dominant figure who becomes the wise one in her old age. It's a matriarchal society, you know.

But the Navajo woman never demands her status. She achieves, earns, accomplishes it through maturity. That maturing process is psychological. It has to do with one's feelings for the land and being a part of the whole cycle of nature. It's difficult to explain to a non-Indian . . .

Envy and jealousy, to the maturing Navajo woman, are the most harmful of all the diseases and the most self-destructive. Also taboo is a woman who speaks out . . . always the words must be carefully chosen, especially in giving advice or in putting another in his place without hurting his feelings.

It is brazenly immodest for a Navajo woman to look someone else in the eye until she is at least forty-five years of age . . . and has earned the maturity and the right to look into the mirrors of another's soul.

Old people are to be revered for their wisdom, their experience and their on-going teachings . . . they are not to be shunted aside or put away.

LOVE, GRANDMA

LOIS BISSELL JIRCITANO

Gently traced,
this hand of bark-dry grooves
lies on fels naptha sheets
not a sacred relic
but a legacy of strength.

its last will and testament reads:

that when she delivered him
into the gentle hands of the shaman
she asked for his moccasins
so he couldn't leave without her.

they laughed together
but he left and walked
the cold journey alone,
and she bore the weight
of the family tree.

now as i sit in haunched acceptance
  i feel my share of the future
descend from those hands so,
          gently traced.

5.

WHERE DO WE FIND JUSTICE IN AMERICA?

IT'S ALMOST SELF-GOVERNMENT
LILA MCCORTNEY NISQUALLY-QUINAULT

We're not living like our ancestors did. We're living like non-Indians. Anyone that's read history sees the difference. We can't expect too much from the government. Some reservations think the government done them wrong. But really, it was just poor management through our agencies. I don't speak for other tribes. But for the Quinault, the government has done right by them. The government took the land, but we got settlements. It's the Indians' own fault if they sold—they weren't forced to.

There's plenty of resources: fishing, clam-digging, shale-cutting, and shaker mills. A few of the boys depend on fishing for a living; fortunately we have two rivers. We stay pretty much within our boundaries. We've been to court several times against the state about the steelheads.[1] We have a business committee. Once a year we have an annual meeting, a general council where we take our business matters. It's almost self-government.

[1] Sports interests stock the river with steelheads, which attract white fishermen. The Indians view this as an intrusion in their waters.

I HAVE A HOUSE AND A FEW SHACKS
LAURA ZIEGLER BRULÉ SIOUX

The BIA has turned everything over to the tribe. So if you stand in with the members of the council and the chairman, you can get someplace. But if you don't, well you're just out of luck. We have white people working here. They all have good jobs. But some of the Indian people have to leave the reservation to get a job . . .

I have a house and a few shacks. A tornado went through. Broke all of my windows out and everything. But OEO [Office of Economic Opportunity] is fixing it up and I'm thankful for that. Should be done soon. They're going to put in a toilet and everything.

THE OBSTACLES WE FACE
WINIFRED JOURDAIN OJIBWE (CHIPPEWA)

Ms. Jourdain is chairperson of the Upper Midwest Indian Center in Minneapolis. She has maintained strong ties to the White Earth Reservation community where she was born.

You have to be Indian to know the obstacles we face. There's still discrimination against Indians. They're the last hired and the first to be laid off. Indian people have never been given a chance.

Whites have been allowed to lease land on our reservations and put up resorts. But it's the whites who benefit; very few of our people have been put to work. A snowmobile factory was established on the White Earth Reservation. Tribal officials took $17.50 out of each check the people received from the government as a payment for their land. The factory was supposed to provide jobs for the poor people on the reservation. But the jobs and profit went to the few powerful families who dominate the reservation.[2]

It's the same with the government housing programs. They've been mismanaged. Those in power point to the really run-down homes and ask for government funds. But the have-nots don't get the new homes. And the scholarships don't go to the people who really need them. There are people in government who have tried to help us. But they can't fight the system.

When I go up to the reservation, the people tell me these things. But they won't write it down. They're afraid of being abused. And the newspapers don't tell what is really happening. Down here in the city there's a BIA office. The majority of Indians live off the reservation. But the BIA isn't interested in them. The services are oriented for Indians who have remained on the reservations.

CAN I SAY DOLLY BIRD

Native Americans have long protested the insensitivity of the government bureaucracy with which they have had to contend, and the official neglect. They ask for recognition of their culture and their humanity.

And it's hard to see the mountains
when you're sitting in the subway
It's hard I said to feel the wind
When you're waiting in some welfare office
but I'm not a case, I'm not a number

[2] The factory, according to Ms. Jourdain, is no longer in operation.—J. K.

I can do quillwork
Mister, I can ride with no
saddle and hey, listen
my brother with his own carved
arrows can stalk a deer.
Why? are you checking boxes
when I am trying to talk   no
I do not have outside income
but there is a tall
cottonwood I know and sometimes
I go to see the leaves and this
morning I heard a meadowlark
 when is the end. . . . to die is not the end
 when is the end. . . . to die is not the end.
he said, I made my ears like a fox stand
to hear and I never even go in
a bank so I got no account
There is an old man I heard
saying, "make moccasins . . ."
no he does not give me money, he
said to the people
"make moccasins for your children, it
is time to go" and I guess we are going
on the plains south where you are always facing
many winters wise. I want someday to bring
when the sun makes white sparks on
the creek like dancing fires, I
want to bring some *kinnikinnik* to him
he remembers the red willow smoke and a
buckskin bag and why do your eyes
say I tell lies?
I never been insane, I
never been in jail, I do not drink, I am not
an addict. I have no car, I do
not have syphilis or cavities, I did
have TB, I did drop out, and I
did get fired, I did not commit mail fraud, I

did not overthrow the government (lately)
with your pencil flying, mister,
can I say there is a good red road
and a sacred hoop of our people
which was broken but I would like
to help mend so the old man would
be happy. My brother
brought fresh meat to him
but the old man says there is not
much time before he will feed the wolves
I want him to know that the
rivers run free—I do not have
a pen to sign here—the forests grow
tall, the plains—I was just in my mind
thinking mister during this investigation—
of the plains where the dirt is living
and wild horses disappear behind a hill,
I wanted to see the old man at dawn stand
on the living plains with his
horse near, see him raise his
arms to the sun, hear him say
"Thank you father"

. . . again

DON'T SEE NO WINGS ON WHITE PEOPLE
GRACE BLACK ELK OGLALA SIOUX

An Indian reservation has been compared to a colonial system. Power, in the view of some Indians, is too often in the hands of an elite clique dominated by the Bureau of Indian Affairs. White influence is felt in the schools, churches, and other reservation institutions. Grace Black Elk, long active in the resistance on the Pine Ridge Reservation in South Dakota, gives her view of Indian/white relations.

Grace Black Elk. Photograph by Michael Shuster.

So they want to convert us to Catholic, Episcopal, all that trash, and believe in the Bible and go to a place where they call heaven, and if we don't we go to hell, and so on. So the Indian's supposed to lay down his weapons and be converted into Christian way. No more savage, he's gonna be a Christian. I guess he'll grow some wings right away, so he can be equal to the white men. But I don't see no wings on white people.

I don't think the white people really care for each other. Like if you're hungry, you can't go into a café and get a free meal. You have to pay for it. Like these people, for an example, yesterday there was a woman that lost her boy here. Her only son—she lost him. And she bought a lot of groceries to come and feed us here. She has it in her heart for Indian people. That's the way Indian people are. They'd rather give than be greedy and take everything away from other people. . . .

Well, if they call themselves Christians and they really believe in that Bible, put their religion ahead of their APCs[3] and all their guns. But they're just using that Bible as a mask. Every Sunday they go to church, and then Monday morning they stand in line making machine guns and tanks and H-bombs and nuclear heads and all that. . . .

You know, everything's white man's law. *Everything.* What if it was the other way around? Like I asked one policeman over in Scottsbluff. I said, "Do we have to go under white man's law all the time? You're not the only race here on earth. There's the black race, there's yellow race, there's red race, and there's white race. But it seems like we always have to bend to your will, bend to white people and their laws, man-made laws."

Yes, if he means peace on earth like he's been saying, he has to recognize the red man as a nation. That's the only way he'll gain peace. Because the Great Spirit created four divisions, that's the white, black, yellow, and red race, and he cannot bar the red man anymore. He'd like to keep us down, kick us down, keep us under

[3] *APCs:* Armored personnel carriers.

his thumb, and keep us on reservations, but he cannot do that anymore.

Like I said, our ancestors used to go to Washington, D.C., going to talk to the president, whoever happens to be president. They go up there with what they call grievances, they go up there to accomplish something, which they never do. They just go up there and take pictures with them and come back, they pat them on their back and "The Congress will look into it and in two years you'll get what you want"—and that's all bullshit. Because after the chief leaves they tear it up and throw it in the wastebasket. And they forget about it and they think we forget about it. But we're not going to.

I saw a sign on the door, it says, "The Indians would rather die standing up than be on their knees forever." And that's where they've been keeping us, on our knees. All the time. Keeping us in poverty.

ON MY RESERVATION, WE'RE POOREST OF THE POOR
WINYANWASTÉ OGLALA SIOUX

An 1868 treaty promised to reserve valuable Dakota lands for the Sioux, but today, on the Pine Ridge Reservation, Indians cultivate less than one percent of their land. The rest is leased by white ranchers at minimal fees; the leases are negotiated and approved by the BIA. Winyanwasté is a widow and the mother of eight children. The oldest Indian to take part in the six-day occupation of the BIA in Washington, D.C., in December 1972, she hitchhiked there alone from South Dakota to protest exploitation of Indian land. "We want our original treaties to be recognized," she said. Winyanwasté said that her name means "Good Woman" in Sioux.

On my reservation, we're poorest of the poor. Some of us have to hitchhike to [the town of] Pine Ridge, fifty miles away, to get our business done, while the bureaucrats ride around in nice, empty cars. All our land is under trust for us—we can't do nothing with it ourselves. We can't farm it without permission, or rent it—they think we're so incompetent that we can't do nothing without them.

The money I earn [thirty-five dollars a week as a baby-sitter] is not enough. I need at least fifty dollars and just can't get it. If I had say-so over my own land, maybe I could rent part of it to make up the difference, but I can't.

I hope something good will come out of it [the demonstration]. We brought in a program of twenty points. Nine of them have been met so far, and the others are in negotiation. It was the only way, what we did. We couldn't get through before—this was the only way of getting to the head guards. At least we were heard.

What happens now? I don't know. We're going to go home, go back to our jobs and our daily lives and hope we've done something worthwhile for the Indians of the United States, Canada, and Alaska. I hope something comes out of it.

What if life doesn't change at Pine Ridge? I've lived there all my life. That's where my home is and that's where I'm gonna die.

WE LEARNED TO HATE ONE ANOTHER
IRMA ROOKS OGLALA SIOUX

The town of Wounded Knee on the Pine Ridge Reservation is historically a place of bitter memories. There, hundreds of unarmed Indians were gunned down by United States forces in 1890. In February 1973, members of the Independent Oglala Nation[4] *and the American Indian Movement occupied the town to protest corruption in reservation governments and the lack of self-determination. Federal troops threw a roadblock around the town. Irma Rooks was one of the Oglala Sioux women who broke through the lines. She talked later to*

[4] Those Oglala Sioux who sought the removal of the tribal government then in power. They accused it of rubber-stamping BIA policies and of using intimidation and brutality to stifle opposition.

reporters from Akwesasne Notes *about the government's failure to live up to its treaties with Indian peoples.*

And we all know what the government promised the Indians, and that they never kept the promises . . . They were supposed to help the Indians develop themselves, but they never give them the chance. If we go and try to make a loan, for instance, to make a start, we are not accepted because we are a "ward of the government." This ward of the government is something really terrible because you can't make a bank loan, you can't do anything. You have to get permission from the tribal council; then your tribal council don't approve it and then you can't get anything. Mostly the people that are part Indian and part white get the best, but not the full bloods. Full bloods never get anything.

Some of our tribal representatives are hiding out because they're scared. They're speaking out for the Indians, now they're hiding out. They can't live in fear for the rest of their lives. Something has got to give. I think it's really important that the Government start waking up and listening to the people. Because what the people want in here is what other people need too, to have a better form of government. Not being scared and hiding at nights. That just don't go with a lot of people.

One of my grandfathers got killed here and that's one reason I get down on whites. We know all the stories about it because we were told exactly how it happened. It's been handed down throughout the reservation, like I said about the treaties, handed down to the children as they were growing up. The older people talk about it, and they talk about a lot of things that they used to have, the way they lived long ago, before the white man came. They were kind to each other, helping each other, watching out for each other. They were all related. But after the white man came they started teaching them the white man's way. We learned to hate one another. . . .

The white people that are rich and higher up think they can rule the ones that are lower than they are. But the only thing they have that they worship is their money, the dollar sign. The minority groups, the poor people, know that there is a god, because that's the only thing that they have.

THERE WERE NO MERCY FOR CHILDREN
GLADYS BISSONETTE OGLALA SIOUX

Gladys Bissonette was at Wounded Knee in 1973, serving as negotiator between the Independent Oglala Nation and the government. She saw many people close to her killed or wounded there. As a defense witness in the 1974 trial of occupation leaders, Ms. Bissonette described a fire fight during which FBI agents' bullets struck a church where she and other women were preparing breakfast.

Yes, the firing was heavy. Our little church was just riddled. We had to stay near the floor; no one moved. And this was the first time my little boy ever prayed, my little twelve-year-old boy. I knew there was something wrong, so I tried to talk to him.

There were a lot of those people inside of there, mostly women, girls, and I think my little boy was the youngest one there. And the firing got so bad, and it got worse, and our church, we just kept getting firing on it, you know, and there was a radio on in the kitchen we could hear voices on and what they were saying about the fire fight. We could hear over the radio where they were shooting gas into the AIM bunkers.

All I have in mind as I lay on the floor was how they could paralyze our boys and come down on the women and children. As I remember back on days when they had unarmed our ancestors, killed them and let them freeze to death, there were no mercy for children. There were no mercy for the women . . .

I didn't care for myself because I knew what I was standing up for. I was standing up for justice for the Indian people, but I

Gladys Bissonette. Photograph courtesy *Minneapolis Star*, 1974.

just couldn't bear to think of the older women and the small children, who still have a full life ahead of them. It was around four o'clock when the firing finally stopped . . .

Every time us women gathered to protest or demonstrate, they always aim machine guns at us. Women and children. I would like to know why they would shoot us Indians down just to save a building. Take human lives to save a building? How greedy can you get?

We do not know anything about conspiracy. The Indians are guided by the Great Spirit and our sacred pipe. So we look into whatever we think is right . . .

We do not intend to commit crimes. If there's a crime against looking for justice, where do we go to find justice here in America?

WHITE-INDIAN CONFRONTATION

VIRGINIA DRIVING HAWK SNEVE ROSEBUD SIOUX

Following the occupation of Wounded Knee, factionalism escalated on the Pine Ridge Reservation, as did violent clashes between Indians and whites. Ms. Sneve, a free-lance writer from South Dakota wrote in the Indian Historian: "*. . . American Indian Movement leaders . . . have become spokesmen for the Indians within the state . . . But the people in the center of the controversy and turmoil, the Indian and non-Indian citizens of South Dakota, are ignored.*"

. . . The reservation was once a good place to raise children. The closeness of family, comradeship of friends, the slow pace, the sparse, lonely beauty of the land once compensated for the lack of material necessities. Now neighbors and friends, be they Indian or white, look at each other with distrust . . .

There is still bigotry and racism among many white people in

South Dakota. But there is also intolerance and hatred among Indians against whites, full bloods against mixed-bloods and vice versa.

And there is ignorance. White children, even in South Dakota, still believe Indians wear feathers and are bloodthirsty savages. This view reflects the attitudes and misconceptions of generations of stereotyping in literature and the media. But headline-making violence on reservations reinforces the concept.

Violence, conflict, and white-Indian confrontation delight the journalist. The quiet efforts of many to better the situation are not noticed. Universities and the public school systems are making an honest effort to remedy the wrongs of the past, with Indian studies and language courses. Public television in South Dakota is making an attempt to explore and present Indian history and contemporary life. The state government is making a positive move with its Indian Task Force to understand and deal with the problems of Indian citizens.

Unknown to the world are the hundreds of Indians and non-Indians who live peacefully as neighbors, who play, work, and worship together. This harmonious coexistence of respect for each others' values and needs must be recognized. It is the only way.

THE BRAVE-HEARTED WOMEN

SHIRLEY HILL WITT   AKWESASNE MOHAWK

The government's charges against the two leading Wounded Knee defendants were dismissed. In January 1976, a new administration, pledged to governmental reform, was elected at Pine Ridge, giving the people hope. But according to Shirley Hill Witt, regional director of the United States Commission on Civil Rights in Denver, there was no end to "battlefield sexism, the targeting of women by law enforcement officers and vigilantes." She wrote in Akwesasne Notes *of the death of a young Canadian woman who had been active in the occupation.*

. . . On February 24, 1976, the body of a young woman was found where it had lain for many days and nights along the highway north of Wanblee on the Pine Ridge Reservation. The coroner contacted by the BIA declared that death was caused by exposure, that is, natural causes.

FBI agents severed the hands from the body. They said they had to send them to the Washington office for identification. A week later, the body was buried in an unmarked grave at the Holy Rosary Mission. By that time, however, the identity of the young woman was known and communicated to family and then to friends. They insisted on an exhumation and a second autopsy. This time, the independent autopsy read differently, the horror of its statement blotting through its precise language: ". . . Removed (from the brain) is a metallic pellet dark gray in color grossly consistent with lead."

The traditional leaders of Oglala released the following statement about her death before the second autopsy was performed:

". . . We want to know the truth about Anna Mae's death and the possibility of the government's involvement in it. Anna Mae Pictou was respected and loved by the people of Oglala. We mourn her and we urge all law-abiding citizens to demand the real truth about her death."

March 14, 1976, dawned windy, flinging snow upon those who had come to bury Anna Mae Pictou Aquash. "Creation was unhappy," one woman said . . .

Some women had driven from Pine Ridge the night before—a very dangerous act—"to do what needed to be done." Young women dug the grave. A ceremonial tipi was set up . . . A woman seven months pregnant gathered sage and cedar to be burned in the tipi. Young AIM members were the pallbearers: they laid her on pine boughs while religious leaders spoke the sacred words and performed the ancient duties. People brought presents for Anna Mae to take with her to the Spirit World. They also brought presents for her two sisters to carry back to Nova Scotia with them to give to her orphaned daughters.

The executioners of Anna Mae did not snuff out a meddlesome woman. They exalted a Brave-Hearted Woman for all time . . .

Among the Iroquois, it is the women who decide when the people will go to war, because when the war is done, it is the women who weep. Will the Brave-Hearted Women decide that, with Anna Mae's death, the war is over? Or will they decide . . . "We're struggling for our life. We're struggling to survive as a people."

Anna Mae Pictou Aquash faces the sun's first light with the white, black, red, and yellow streamers flapping overhead on poles placed in the Four Sacred Directions cornering her grave.

GASIFICATION: THE NAVAJO WILL BE SUBMERGED

CLAUDEEN ARTHUR NAVAJO

Strip mining proposed for the Four Corners area of the Navajo Nation will affect thousands of acres of Navajo land. Water now used for irrigation will be diverted to gasification plants which convert coal into synthetic gas. Outside workers will be brought in. "The Navajo will be submerged," says Claudeen Arthur, attorney. "Many do not have lights or indoor plumbing, yet they must give up their land to provide fuel for distant cities. They are losing so much. They are part of the land." In hearings before the U.S. Bureau of Reclamation, Ms. Arthur has raised complex issues "affecting the lives of people."

. . . Of particular concern are those Navajo persons whose very lives will be most directly affected by the proposed plants, those persons who . . . must be relocated . . . and those whose grazing rights are taken without relocation . . .

The devastation caused by the proposed plants will be such that, in fact, those families must be moved . . . the families to be moved are those who might be classified as traditional Navajo families whose primary source of livelihood is the grazing of livestock. . . . Where will the families be moved to? Every square mile of the Navajo Reservation is presently burdened beyond its capacity. . . . Moving additional families onto land already severely overgrazed would cause untold havoc . . .

The Bureau of Reclamation's Environmental Impact Statement says "complete restoration of the land surface is unlikely"; then will grazing be provided for these families indefinitely because their removal would then be permanent? . . .

Paying the families the monetary value of their hogans, corrals, sheds, etc., is not compensating them for their loss of livelihood, or for the loss of that intangible "central place in the sacred world," which is the way of life of a traditional Navajo family.

A HUGE GAS CHAMBER
MARIA SANCHEZ CHEYENNE

Strip mining is also planned for the Crow Reservation and the Northern Cheyenne in Montana. Tribal people charge that the emissions from the coal stacks contain sulfur dioxide, which is held in layers in the earth. Maria Sanchez reminded a conference of church leaders that, as shareholders in the energy companies, they had a responsibility to prevent "the totality of genocide."

I am the mother of nine children. My concern is for their future, for their children, and for future generations. As a woman, I draw strength from the traditional spiritual people. . . .

The oil and coal companies are building a huge gas chamber for the Northern Cheyennes.

WE'RE TALKING ABOUT CULTURAL GENOCIDE
RAMONA BENNETT PUYALLUP

Despite a long-standing treaty affirming the Northwest tribes' rights to take fish from their coastal waters, native fishermen have long been harassed by commercial and sport fishermen who, with state support, challenge their claims. In a 1970 interview recorded by Akwesasne Notes, *tribal leader Ramona Bennett gave her view of the struggle. Although a district court ruled in favor of the Indians in 1974, opposition and violence continue in the state of Washington.*

At this time, our people are fighting to preserve their last treaty right—the right to fish. We lost our land base.[5] There is no game in the area . . . We're dependent not just economically but culturally on the right to take fish. Fishing is part of our art forms and religion and diet, and the entire culture is based around it. And so when we talk about [the white man's] ripping off the right to take fish, we're talking about cultural genocide.

A lot of people are dependent on fishing for a livelihood, but we're being squeezed out by the commercial fishing industry, which is really powerful in that area. Everything comes back to money. This is a monetary society, with really funny values. The industry has flooded the market with frozen fish.

The Treaty ratified in 1854 expressed very clearly that our people caught fish; it was processed, that is, smoked, then used for barter and trade for a livelihood. Our people have fought a

[5] Surrendered by treaty in exchange for the right to fish forever.

legal battle for more than forty-nine years . . . Our resource [the salmon] is being depleted . . . Our people at hearings have made statements that when the fish come into the river, they meet pollution and they meet the industry's fishermen. And when they get upstream, they meet dams . . . They find that the spawning grounds have been interfered with by the lumber company and the eggs die . . . The state is blaming the loss of the resource on the Indians. They can't blame the commercial industry because it's too powerful, so they hang it on Indian people. They say those Indians are down there with nets catching all the fish. Fisheries law enforcement agents come out with the tactical squad, and just run right over the people with high-powered boats. They push the people to the bank of the river and pound them around. This has gone on for nineteen years. Finally, we said this is enough. We said we were not going to tolerate any more arrests, we were not going to tolerate any more confiscation of gear. An injunction said the state has the right to regulate us for conservation purposes . . .

We set up a camp for security—no arms whatsoever. There was another arrest. Finally, one of the boys went down to the river to fish, and his mother went up on the bank. And she said: "This boy is nineteen years old and we've been fighting on this river for as many years as he's been alive. And no one is going to pound my son around, no one is going to arrest him. No one is going to touch my son or I'm going to shoot them." And she had a rifle. "If I shoot, I want everyone to stand back. I don't want to be mistaken for a mob. I am one woman with one gun, and no one is going to touch my son."

Then we did have an armed camp in the city of Tacoma. . . . If we gave up our arms, the government would immediately lose interest in us . . . We had every right in the world to be there. We were on federal trust land. If anyone should be maintaining control on that river protecting resources the Indians should have the authority to do it. They lived there for 35,000 years, and the fish always came back. And the white people have only been there for eighty years and every year they're afraid there aren't going to be any more fish. And yet they have the gall to question our people's conscience in the area of fishing and control, and our responsibility to resources. You know, we don't plan on going anyplace else. This is our home . . . White people simply can't understand having roots and having a responsibility toward the earth.

They came right on the reservation with a force of three hundred people. They gassed us, they clubbed people around, they laid $125,000 in bail on us. At that time I was a member of the Puyallup Tribal Council, and I was a spokesman for the camp. And I told them what our policy was: that we were there to protect our Indian fishermen. And because I used the voice-gun, I'm being charged with inciting a riot. I'm faced with an eight-year sentence.

They gathered up everyone. They even arrested our animals. They packed up the tipis. Then they brought in bulldozers. And we had a smokehouse and a kitchen. And they bulldozed all of our land. This is Indian land; this is a reservation. They came on with bulldozers and they wiped out all signs of life. Which is I think what they intend to do with the tribe—to totally extinguish it. There should be no evidence other than a few arrowheads and baskets in museums.

Everybody likes Indians . . . everybody likes beads and feathers. But when you get down to real flesh-and-blood, honest-to-God Indians who may have rickets or tuberculosis or some really serious problems, then they're not liked anymore.

THE POWER CAME FROM THE PEOPLE
ADA DEER MENOMINEE

In the 1790s, the War Department initiated services for Indian tribes in order to "civilize" them. In 1934, Indians won the legal right to administer their own federal programs; still the bureaucrats dictated policy. Today the government is gradually shedding some of its paternalism toward Indians. Educator, social worker, and tribal leader Ada Deer tells how the Menominee challenged the system and won a battle for tribal autonomy.

I was born on the Menominee reservation in Wisconsin, and lived there for eighteen years. As a teen-ager I saw the poverty of the people—poor housing, poor education, poor health. I thought, "This isn't the way it should be. People should have a better life."

I wanted to help the tribe in some way, but I wanted to have something to offer. I decided that going to college and developing my skills was the best way to break out of the bonds of poverty. After college, I entered law school.

In 1961 the tribe was terminated; that is, federal support was withdrawn. Some of us opposed termination from the start, but we were overruled. Only five percent of the people voted; they were lured by the cash payments offered in return for giving up government services. Most of the people were uninformed; they did not protest termination because they did not foresee its drastic implications. The government pushed it through without preparing the people. It was "an experiment."

The years 1961–1973 were a political, economic, and cultural disaster for the Menominee. Formerly, under the tribal system everyone had been equal, with one vote per tribal member. Under the new corporate structure just a few people had the power to make decisions.

We were the state's poorest county, with just one small industry, a lumber mill. We were suddenly faced with massive tax burdens. Our hospital and school were forced to close. The people suffered a great deal. To survive, the tribe had to sell some of its land.

Land is very dear to the Menominee. We have a beautiful reservation—over 234,000 acres of mountains, streams, and lakes. Our reservation is our homeland, guaranteed by a treaty. Our cultural identity is bound to the land.

With termination, many of the people moved to the cities in

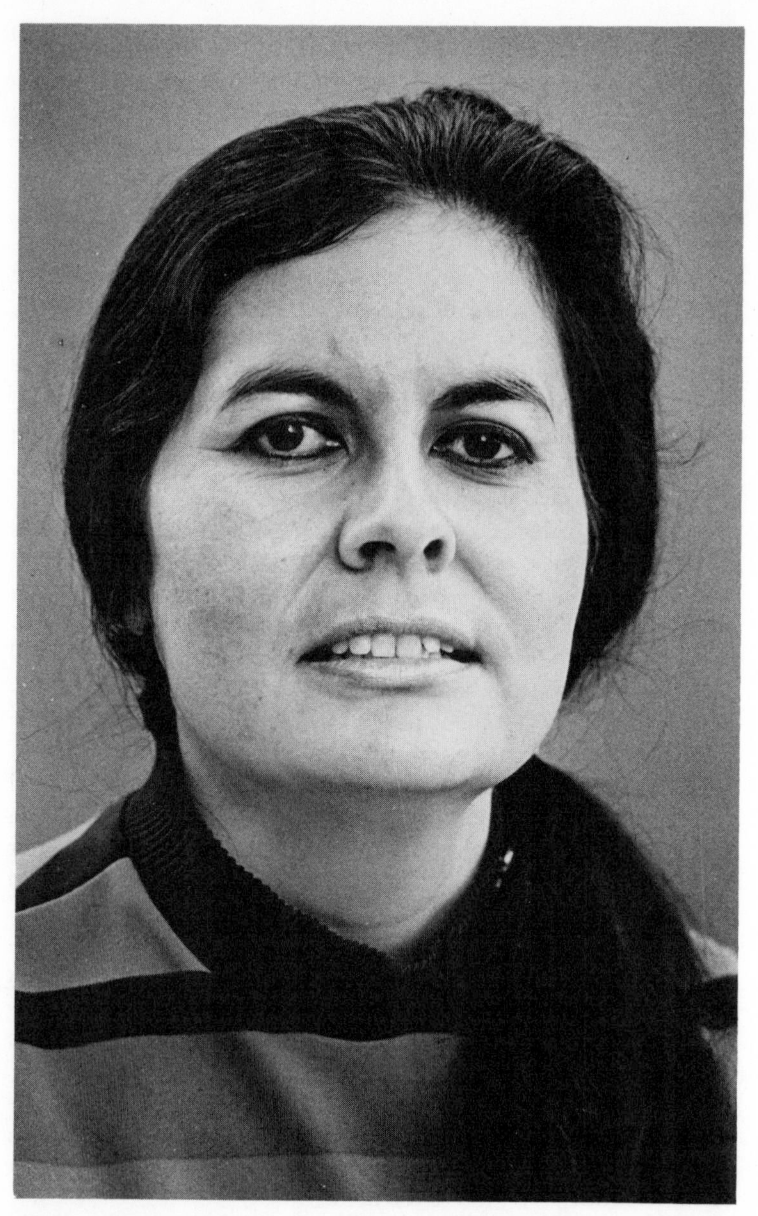

Ada Deer. Photograph courtesy *Wisconsin State Journal*.

search of jobs. They lost their connection with their traditional culture and way of life. Then too, termination canceled tribal membership for children born after 1954.

The government had tried for two hundred years to eliminate the Indians. They tried wars, disease, putting us on reservations. They tried acculturation—shipping us off to cities. Termination was the ultimate expression of that . . .

I wanted to get involved. People said I was too young, too naïve—you can't fight the system. I dropped out of law school. That was the price I had to pay to get involved. It was worth it.

In 1970 we started our movement called DRUMS.[6] We sought an end to land sales, the restoration of federal support, and full participation of the people in tribal government. To present our goals to our congressman, we staged a march covering one hundred and fifty miles from our reservation to Madison. Our congressman said he didn't think our legislation had much of a chance, but he'd introduce it.

I spent six months in Washington influencing congressmen and mobilizing the support of our people throughout the country. We were able to get our legislation through the House of Representatives 404 to 3; an exciting day. It went through the Senate on a voice vote with no protest and was signed into law on December 1, 1973. The land was restored to trust status; roles in government were opened to young people and to women.

Where did the manpower and womanpower come from to accomplish this? It came from the people. Men and women working together as a total community. Now we Indian people believe we can do anything!

[6] *DRUMS:* Determination of Rights and Unity for Menominee Shareholders.

6.

TO WALK IN BEAUTY

ONCE AGAIN
LIZ SOHAPPY PALOUSE

Om-na-ma, *Ms. Sohappy's Palouse name, means "stopping on a hill and looking down." After earning her tuition by picking cherries and working in a fruit warehouse, she attended the Institute of American Indian Arts, and studied art in Portland. Ms. Sohappy is a member of the Yakima tribal group and is from Toppenish, Washington.*

Let go of the present and death.
Go to the place nearest the stars,
gather twigs, logs;
build a small fire,
a huge angry fire.

Gather nature's skin,
wet it, stretch it,
make a hard drum,
fill it with water
to muffle the sound.

Gather dry leaves, herbs,
feed into the fire.
Let the smoke rise
up to the dark sky,
to the roundness of the sun.

Moisten your lips,
loosen your tongue,
let the chant echo
from desert, to valley, to peak—
wherever your home may be.

Remember the smoke,
the chants, the drums,
the stick grandfather held
as he spoke in the dark
of the power of his fathers?

Gather your memories
into a basket, into a pot,
into your cornhusk bag, and
grandfather is alive
for us to see once again.

TO PRESERVE THE OLD WAY

WAHLEAH LUJAN TAOS

For centuries, the land around Blue Lake served as a sanctuary and religious refuge to the people of the Taos pueblo in New Mexico. Then in 1906, the United States Forest Service appropriated the land for the use of tourists. With fishermen and loggers in the area, its sacred values were lost. The protest, of which Ms. Lujan was a part, was successful. In December 1970, the land was returned to the people.

In the last twenty years we've been pushed around a lot. Our land is being taken away. Our life is being taken away. Our sacred Blue Lake, the church of our Indian religion, is being taken away. Land that has never been used by anyone else. Land that has belonged to no one but us. Land that my people have been on for six hundred and fifty years. And all of a sudden these strange people come in and tell us: You can't use this land any more! It's not yours!

So we needed somebody. We need somebody who would go out and learn to compete with the white man on his level. We have to fight back. So I went out. I did not want to go to college. To go away. But I had to go. . . .

I hope most of all, by venturing out, to show my people one can be modern, and yet be very much part of the old way. In fact, it is becoming necessary to be modern in order to preserve the old way.

DINÉ[1]

PAULA GUNN ALLEN LAGUNA

In past generations, many reservation Navajos traded with outsiders but otherwise kept themselves apart, thus appearing impassive, inviolate. But in their dances and "sings" they shone with an inner light. Today, as in the past, their Yeis, *or masked figures, personify divine powers. They dance to restore harmony within the individual and to ensure his or her proper relationship to natural forces. Paula Gunn Allen grew up in a land-grant town near the Navajo Nation in New Mexico.*

Rainbow
space between earth and sky
defines Yei that bracelet pale arms:
"They sell anything these days," pale woman
peers across the turquoise glass. She
wants to sell me that piece. Her eyes hold

[1] *Diné:* a Navajo word meaning "the people."

a nation's birthright in their gleam, set
in arrogance, the certitude of fools.

Rainbow. Yei dance. Hold
harmony in raising arms: no sign of salvation
but its path: canned peaches, strawberry coke,
taken beneath the blooming boughs of my
        grandfather's tree
in the summers when they came to buy and
        sell and steal
bad children, as grandma used to say. Nose
pressed to gate, I watched them,
hoping I had not been good, so beautiful their way,
those days.

Rainbow, Yei hold
eternity, owned
secret souls raised up: light
way of walking, healing, secret
heart remains still: bodies, hands, clothes shimmering
July afternoon (safe behind grandma's blooming
        fence: "they
must be free. I could walk that way, sometime."

Rainbow, space between silver shining on the shelves,
"Nothing sacred but money to them" she says, trying to show
she knows her patsy, shivering
I turn angry
away.

THE MAN TO SEND RAIN CLOUDS
LESLIE SILKO LAGUNA

It has been said that water is the blood of a pueblo; tradition is its soul. Age-old Pueblo Indians' ceremonies designed to bring rain to the parched desert towns survive to this day. Leslie Silko was born in 1948 on the Laguna Reservation near Albuquerque, New Mexico. In her stories interlaced with native tradition and lore, she links the worlds of yesterday and today.

ONE

They found him under a big cottonwood tree. His Levi jacket and pants were faded light-blue so that he had been easy to find. The big cottonwood tree stood apart from a small grove of winter-bare cottonwoods which grew in the wide, sandy arroyo. He had been dead for a day or more, and the sheep had wandered and scattered up and down the arroyo. Leon and his brother-in-law, Ken, gathered the sheep and left them in the pen at the sheep camp before they returned to the cottonwood tree. Leon waited under the tree while Ken drove the truck through the deep sand to the edge of the arroyo. He squinted up at the sun and unzipped his jacket—it sure was hot for this time of year. But high and northwest the blue mountains were still deep in snow. Ken came sliding down the low, crumbling bank about fifty yards down, and he was bringing the red blanket.

Before they wrapped the old man, Leon took a piece of string out of his pocket and tied a small gray feather in the old man's long white hair. Ken gave him the paint. Across the brown wrinkled forehead he drew a streak of white and along the high cheekbones he drew a strip of blue paint. He paused and watched Ken throw pinches of corn meal and pollen into the wind that fluttered the small gray feather. Then Leon painted with yellow under the old man's broad nose, and finally,when he had painted green across the chin, he smiled.

"Send us rain clouds, Grandfather." They laid the bundle in

Leslie Silko. Photograph courtesy The Viking Press.

the back of the pickup and covered it with a heavy tarp before they started back to the pueblo.

They turned off the highway onto the sandy pueblo road. Not long after they passed the store and post office they saw Father Paul's car coming toward them. When he recognized their faces he slowed his car and waved for them to stop. The young priest rolled down the car window.

"Did you find old Teofilo?" he asked loudly.

Leon stopped the truck. "Good morning, Father. We were just out to the sheep camp. Everything is OK now."

"Thank God for that. Teofilo is a very old man. You really shouldn't allow him to stay at the sheep camp alone."

"No, he won't do that any more now."

"Well, I'm glad you understand. I hope I'll be seeing you at Mass this week—we missed you last Sunday. See if you can get old Teofilo to come with you." The priest smiled and waved at them as they drove away.

TWO

Louise and Teresa were waiting. The table was set for lunch, and the coffee was boiling on the black iron stove. Leon looked at Louise and then at Teresa.

"We found him under a cottonwood tree in the big arroyo near sheep camp. I guess he sat down to rest in the shade and never got up again." Leon walked toward the old man's bed. The red plaid shawl had been shaken and spread carefully over the bed, and a new brown flannel shirt and pair of stiff new Levis were arranged neatly beside the pillow. Louise held the screen door open while Leon and Ken carried in the red blanket. He looked small and shriveled, and after they dressed him in the new shirt and pants he seemed more shrunken.

It was noontime now because the church bells rang the Angelus. They ate the beans with hot bread, and nobody said anything until after Teresa poured the coffee.

Ken stood up and put on his jacket. "I'll see about the gravediggers. Only the top layer of soil is frozen. I think it can be ready before dark."

Leon nodded his head and finished his coffee. After Ken had been gone for a while, the neighbors and clanspeople came quietly to embrace Teofilo's family and to leave food on the table because the gravediggers would come to eat when they were finished.

THREE

The sky in the west was full of pale-yellow light. Louise stood outside with her hands in the pockets of Leon's green army jacket that was too big for her. The funeral was over, and the old men had taken their candles and medicine bags and were gone. She waited until the body was laid into the pickup before she said anything to Leon. She touched his arm, and he noticed that her hands were still dusty from the corn meal that she had sprinkled around the old man. When she spoke, Leon could not hear her.

"What did you say? I didn't hear you."

"I said that I had been thinking about something."

"About what?"

"About the priest sprinkling holy water for Grandpa. So he won't be thirsty."

Leon stared at the new moccasins that Teofilo had made for the ceremonial dances in the summer. They were nearly hidden by the red blanket. It was getting colder, and the wind pushed gray dust down the narrow pueblo road. The sun was approaching the long mesa where it disappeared during the winter. Louise stood there shivering and watching his face. Then he zipped up his jacket and opened the truck door. "I'll see if he's there."

FOUR

Ken stopped the pickup at the church, and Leon got out; and then Ken drove down the hill to the graveyard where people were waiting. Leon knocked at the old carved door with its symbols of the Lamb. While he waited he looked up at the twin bells from the king of Spain with the last sunlight pouring around them in their tower.

The priest opened the door and smiled when he saw who it was. "Come in! What brings you here this evening?"

The priest walked toward the kitchen, and Leon stood with

his cap in his hand, playing with the earflaps and examining the living room—the brown sofa, the green armchair, and the brass lamp that hung down from the ceiling by links of chain. The priest dragged a chair out of the kitchen and offered it to Leon.

"No thank you, Father. I only came to ask you if you would bring your holy water to the graveyard."

The priest turned away from Leon and looked out the window at the patio full of shadows and the dining-room windows of the nuns' cloister across the patio. The curtains were heavy, and the light from within faintly penetrated; it was impossible to see the nuns inside eating supper. "Why didn't you tell me he was dead? I could have brought the Last Rites anyway."

Leon smiled. "It wasn't necessary, Father."

The priest stared down at his scuffed brown loafers and the worn hem of his cassock. "For a Christian burial it was necessary."

His voice was distant, and Leon thought that his blue eyes looked tired.

"It's OK Father, we just want him to have plenty of water."

The priest sank down into the green chair and picked up a glossy missionary magazine. He turned the colored pages full of lepers and pagans without looking at them.

"You know I can't do that, Leon. There should have been the Last Rites and a funeral Mass at the very least."

Leon put on his green cap and pulled the flaps down over his ears. "It's getting late, Father. I've got to go."

When Leon opened the door Father Paul stood up and said, "Wait." He left the room and came back wearing a long brown overcoat. He followed Leon out the door and across the dim churchyard to the adobe steps in front of the church. They both stooped to fit through the low adobe entrance. And when they started down the hill to the graveyard only half of the sun was visible above the mesa.

The priest approached the grave slowly, wondering how they had managed to dig into the frozen ground; and then he remembered that this was New Mexico, and saw the pile of cold loose sand beside the hole. The people stood close to each other with little clouds of steam puffing from their faces. The priest looked at them and saw a pile of jackets, gloves, and scarves in the yellow, dry tumbleweeds that grew in the graveyard. He looked at the red blanket, not sure that Teofilo was so small, wondering if it wasn't some perverse Indian trick—something they did in March to ensure a good harvest—wondering if maybe old Teofilo was actually at sheep camp corraling the sheep for the night. But there he was, facing into a cold dry wind and squinting at the last sunlight, ready to bury a red wool blanket while the faces of his parishioners were in shadow with the last warmth of the sun on their backs.

His fingers were stiff, and it took him a long time to twist the lid off the holy water. Drops of water fell on the red blanket and soaked into dark icy spots. He sprinkled the grave and the water disappeared almost before it touched the dim, cold sand; it reminded him of something—he tried to remember what it was, because he thought if he could remember he might understand this. He sprinkled more water; he shook the container until it was empty, and the water fell through the light from sundown like August rain that fell while the sun was still shining, almost evaporating before it touched the wilted squash flowers.

The wind pulled at the priest's brown Franciscan robe and swirled away the corn meal and pollen that had been sprinkled on the blanket. They lowered the bundle into the ground, and they didn't bother to untie the stiff pieces of new rope that were tied around the ends of the blanket. The sun was gone, and over on the highway the eastbound lane was full of headlights. The priest walked away slowly. Leon watched him climb the hill, and when he had disappeared within the tall, thick walls, Leon turned to look up at the high blue mountains in the deep snow that reflected a faint red light from the west. He felt good because it was finished, and he was happy about the sprinkling of the holy water; now the old man could send them big thunderclouds for sure.

I KNOW WHO I AM
MARGARET VICKERS TSIMSHIAN-KWA GULTH

Ms. Vickers is Coordinator of the Indian Education Resources Center at the University of Victoria in British Columbia. She lectures on Northwest Coast Indian Art at various universities. A young woman of prolific talents, she is also a designer of traditional-contemporary clothing.

I'm working to perpetuate the art forms and design of the Northwest Coast Indians. Our arts—carved totem poles and masks, utensils, songs, and dances—have been with us for thousands of years. It's through our arts that people in this part of the continent are aware of our past, which is our present and which affects our future. Today the old motifs are expressed in contemporary form. A traditional-contemporary art, as I see it.

I'm a member of the Tsimshian-Kwa Gulth Nation. I grew up in Kitkatla, a native Indian village near the mouth of the Skeena River in British Columbia. My people once depended almost entirely on the sea for their livelihood. In fact, *Kitkatla* means "people of the sea."

I'm a half-breed, and most people react sympathetically to that. Actually, there are so many misconceptions. We're not all the "lost generation" or "people in turmoil." At least, I'm not. I've always known my roots. I have a close identification with my parents, their parents, their songs, stories, and crests. I know who my ancestors were, and I know who I am.

There's so much talk about the "rebirth" of our cultural heritage. That's another misconception. It has never left us. People speak of our pride and our dignity in the past tense. We've always had it. And we always will, as long as we respect ourselves and other living beings. Generations ago, our people were taught early in life to respect all persons, plants, and other animals. We were taught that if one disturbed the balance in nature the whole life cycle would begin to change.

I look backward at some of the sad things that have happened to Indian people. Physically, the early explorers and pioneers brought diseases that we had no way of combating. Spiritually and psychologically too, we were besieged. Whole generations were told they were inferior; they tried to forget who they were—to fit into the dominant culture. They resorted to alcohol and drugs, which were too readily available. They lost the battle with themselves.

I feel for people who have gone through that. They've allowed their self-awareness to be confused.

Within each of us there is a struggle between traditional values and new life-styles. But we can deal with that. You can be in the the largest city on earth. As long as you remember who you are you'll never be lost. You'll find peace within yourself.

AFTER HE DIED

PITSEOLAK ASHOONA CAPE DORSET ESKIMO

In her 1972 autobiography, Pitseolak recalled her husband's death from a strange illness: "Many people died in the camps . . . There was no doctor then." Of her seventeen children, only six survived. Still she said, "The old life was a hard life but it was good . . . I think I am a real artist; I draw the old ways."

After my husband died, I felt very alone and unwanted; making prints is what has made me happiest since he died. I am going to keep on doing them until they tell me to stop. If no one tells me to stop, I shall make them as long as I am well. If I can, I'll make them even after I am dead.

WALK IN BEAUTY
MARY MOREZ NAVAJO

Born on the Navajo reservation, artist Mary Morez underwent painful hip surgery as a young child. Years later, she watched her beloved husband, an archaeologist, die a slow and painful death. Her response to this experience: "I don't know why he was taken. Yet so many others are left." Although she was then an established artist, Ms. Morez volunteered her time at the Phoenix Indian Medical Center: "I wanted to go down and just hold those children," she said.

We're not stoic. Where did that stereotype come from? We Navajo cry with joy and sorrow together. We help each other. We feel close even when we are far apart in distance.

We know love because we feel it. Some people talk of love all their lives but never get or give it and therefore really don't know it.

But love learned at the feet of the old people and from the innocence of little children—that day-by-day lesson in feeling love, not just talking about it—is one of the things that makes a hogan more than a physical home.

When I grow old, I want to know I've left something behind. Not as an artist, but as a human being who loves and cares and tends and helps other human beings. To do that is to walk in beauty.

WHERE MOUNTAINLION LAID DOWN WITH DEER
LESLIE SILKO LAGUNA

I climb the black rock mountain
stepping from day to day
silently.
I smell the wind for my ancestors
pale blue leaves
crushed wild mountain smell.
Returning
up the gray stone cliff
where I descended
a thousand years ago.
Returning to faded black stone
where mountainlion laid down with deer.

It is better to stay up here
watching wind's reflection
in tall yellow flowers.
The old ones who remember me are gone
the old songs are all forgotten
and the story of my birth.
How I danced in snow-frost moonlight
distant stars to the end of the Earth,
How I swam away
in freezing mountain water
narrow mossy canyon tumbling down
out of the mountain
out of deep canyon stone
down
the memory
spilling out
into the world.

Drawing of Eskimo woman. Photograph courtesy National Film Board of Canada.

7.

IN A GENTLE WHIRLWIND I WAS SHAKEN, MADE TO SEE ON EARTH IN MANY WAYS

HOW I CAME TO BE A GRADUATE STUDENT

WENDY ROSE HOPI

Ms. Rose was born in 1948 in California's Bay Area. She is the author of Hopi Roadrunner Dancing, Long Division: A Tribal History, *and* Lost Copper. *Currently a graduate student in anthropology at the University of California, Berkeley, she writes: "Much of my recent work deals with coping with being an Indian anthropologist in a discipline that does not welcome Indian people as equals. I feel very alone."*

It was when my songs became quiet.
No one was threatened, no eyes kept locked
on my red hands to see if
they would steal the beads and silver
from museum shelves.
When I became, in the owl's way, a hunter,
they trusted the microscope that hid me
in the grass, that bent up and over me,
too big to drive away. That's how they knew
they could move in.
Those quiet songs, I could tell you,
simply expose the stone spirit

of Warrior Katcina,[1] dancing sideways
through the village; or I could say
that the brave and ragged meat of me
is being tongued away by a foreign god.
I am shut away without food
in a pueblo where everyone has died,
and when it looks like I may break loose,
they tell me I'm *moving* now and
congratulations. All the time my stone spirit song
grows and erupts and laps over the world; my legs roll away
like water on stone and come to where the songs all meet
in ancient matrix, uprooting every spring, and
moving on. It's that kind of moving
from grave to grave.

REFUSE TO BE A VICTIM
BUFFY SAINTE-MARIE (CANADIAN) CREE

Ms. Sainte-Marie was born on the Cree Reservation in Saskatchewan, Canada. She was adopted and brought up by a white family in the United States.

Truth for me has been a wandering path that's crisscrossed all the shades of ecstasy, all the shadows of bitterness.

My heart leaps when I look into the face of my beautiful Indian child, wrapped in the strength of his father's arms: together, we are the flag of North America. We're growing free and joyful.

But the same day, my teeth clench in horror at our history, what's been done to us, what's going on still today, what's in store for us by virtue of our Indianness.

[1] *Katcina:* in Hopi ceremonialism, a masked figure who acts as intermediary between man and god.

I sing the songs of both our summer and our winter. I write throughout all the phases of the moon, because they're all true.

My country is dying, but my nation is healing up. . . .

My mother's father was a great and lovely family man, and a Cree chief. His name was Star Blanket. He knew Sitting Bull of the Sioux, and so did my father's grandfather, Piapot, also a Cree chief. We are Crees, and Sitting Bull was a Sioux. My husband is Sioux, a descendant of Little Crow, and our child is both Cree and Sioux, and I'm proud of us all—Star Blanket, Piapot, Sitting Bull, Little Crow, our parents, our relatives, and ourselves.

You can take an Indian child, hold him by the feet and dunk him in a bucket of whitewash, up and down, day after day, year after year, and it's still only a "maybe" whether or not you'll kill the Indian in him. You might, and you might not. In my case, a white-dipped childhood gave me enough suffocation to show me the difference between breath and death, between Indian sharing values and white gobbledy greed. Day after day, my white-dipped childhood stuck me with little needles, painful little needles piercing me in places where I should have known joy—my heart, my eyes, my woman place, my sleep—giving me little doses of hate regularly, frequently, silently.

So I became immune to the ravages of hate; immune to the disease of the *mooniyasuk*, the whiteman, the *keshagesuk*, the greedy-guts—though it terrified me.

Because I sleep in fear of the blue-eyed Nazi wrapped up in red-white-and-blue, I will never again be caught napping. Because I was attacked, I learned readiness, but what a cost, what a cost!

The whites carry the greed disease. It kills some of them, and most of us. They need to be cured, but they usually don't mind their disease, or even recognize it, because it's all they know and their leaders encourage them in it, and many of them are beyond help. We need strong, healthy medicine, and wise native doctors if we are to survive the plague of the *keshagesuk*—the greed-mad unholy gold-worshipers . . . They've cut themselves off from nature. They dope their children with cornflakes and Chevrolets, and they think they can't live without money. . . .

But their ways are different from ours, Brothers and Sisters. In their eyes, it's all right for them to victimize Indian people, Indian culture, if we stand in the way of their holy quest for a railroad fortune, a gold fortune, an oil fortune, a uranium fortune, a pipeline fortune, a cattle fortune, a water fortune, a political fortune, a fortune in the church, or some other kind of fortune, which they will inevitably call "progress" to dress it up.

But it still comes down to this: if an Indian stands between a *mooniyas* and his money, the Indian is expendable. The teachers, churches, and courts will suddenly effect a double standard, and the Indian will get lost in the shuffle.

Our advantage is that we are used to living skinny. Even if we're full of fry-bread and beans, fat and gas, carbohydrates and malnutrition, we are skinny on the inside. What is skinny? My uncle, Pius Kiasuatum sings me an old Cree song. It goes, "Heyo-hey-ay-oh, my sister-in-law, we are so skinny." It's a strong, sad song that came in wartime.

Skinny can be malnourished, but it's still alive.

Skinny can be bitter, but light and wiry.

Skinny can be tough.

Skinny can be well practiced in the art of living on nothing, nothing to eat, nothing to dream.

Skinny can teach you who your friends are, which pays off in the long run, if you survive—if you don't get to drinking and doping and wasting away your medicine power.

Skinny can be like it used to be—for fasting as one of the steps to finding your vision, if you are a smart Indian and not a stupid victim. . . .

It's self-destructive to save bitterness. Bitterness is meant to be used. It's part of our long-term vision to understand how we've been victimized, but the trick is to break the cycle. . . .

Scream the bloody truth of how we've been raped in every

Buffy Sainte-Marie. Photograph courtesy Vanguard Recording Society, New York.

possible way, and then *rise up and dig the beauty of our people.* Rejoice in our survival and our ways.

MY PEOPLE ARE THE POOR
GLORIA TRUVIDO POMO

A small remnant of the Pomo tribe survives today in California. Ms. Truvido experienced poverty and prejudice as a child, but found her heritage to be her strength.

. . . I wish to accomplish something in life, something of value to my people and other people.

My people are the welfare recipients, the winos who eat in the mission, the people who toil in the fields, the *braceros* who people forget are human beings and tend to think of them as automated machines.

My people are the poor and they are poor and they are rich.

My people are the white trash Okies who are my friends.

My people are the Mexicans who are generous.

My people are the Negroes who took care of me when I was a child.

My people are the Pomo Indians and I am proud.

These are all my people, the only people I know, and I am glad I am part of these human beings, they are the people of life.

Like the Pomo basket made from the roots of the earth I am a strong descendant from the Indians and I will keep my heritage as a Pomo Indian.

It is my essence to fight for equal human rights, so that someday my people will live on this earth as human beings . . .

WE CHOOSE OUR OWN FATE
TSEWAA TEWA

Tsewaa belongs to the Sun Clan of the Tewa Nation at Tesuque pueblo in New Mexico. She has been a leader in the fight to protect and preserve her pueblo's land and water resources. She travels with White Roots of Peace, a group that brings spiritual awareness to native people.

In the beginning, in the beginning we were one people, and our instructions were one.

We had the gift that was our law for life, a law that was known by all from the smallest of insect to the oldest of man . . . We all knew there was only one Creator, so we prayed in the way we were gifted. We were instructed to sing and dance so our crops would grow. We knew the power of the sun, messages of stars, and strength in cold water. We knew everything there is to know so we only had to live according to the cycle as it came . . .

In the beginning was the word. The words that our Grandfathers left are words of instruction . . . how to conduct our lives as man, woman, child, grandmother . . . to benefit our family, community, and nation. Instruction of tasks for our way of life . . .

A simple prayer of thanksgiving was an instruction to all living things. A mourning dove sings a thanksgiving song. A dance, a song, a greeting, a smile was a thanksgiving for life. In the beginning, we knew this prayer because we knew life and we were thankful. Then we knew how to dance, sing, how to smile. Even a man knew how to greet and dance with an ant. We knew, so therefore we lived . . .

Feel the earth, our mother, and grow with her love. Feel the wind, our brother, dust your face with strength. Bathe in the mountain's stream and feel the power it carries. Feel the instructions that are all around and live by them . . .

Now that we've grown away from our mother and her love and care, we are on our own . . . We were not thankful for simple food, simple laws, simple words of communication, simple basic rules. We've complicated our lives and wander now as if we have no instruction to follow.

But remember; there will always be someone who will remember the way, the instruction, the beginning.

And the sun remembered. He carried out his responsibility to his people as he appeared from behind a mountain, from the ocean, or from the flat plains with his instruction. He remembered us, yet how many of us remember him? With him he carries the message of the Grandfathers from the sky world. He carries the children of life. The sun, our Thinking. The sun gave us this day to be born again, to begin again, and a chance to remember. Traveling through time, space, past to future, from childhood to adulthood into the whole cycle of life—we choose our own fate.

THE ENCHANTED OWL
KENOJUAK CAPE DORSET ESKIMO

A shaman once told the Eskimo people that the sun belongs to women. The spirit of the sun takes tangible form in the stonecuts of Kenojuak, a recently widowed mother of five. She draws living creatures enveloped in sunlight; birds spread their wings and flutter in the dance of life. Kenojuak says of *The Enchanted Owl* that the rays of light and swirling tail reach out "to drive away the darkness."

The Enchanted Owl. Stonecut by Kenojuak, 1960.

CHEE'S DAUGHTER
JUANITA PLATERO AND SIYOWIN MILLER NAVAJO

According to the Navajo belief system, the spiritual and material sides of life must be kept in balance. The earth is holy; all of creation is revered. One who turns from the earth and follows the white man's materialistic path will pay a penalty. Chee, a traditional Navajo, loses what he values most. He looks to the land for sustenance, and it does not fail him.

The hat told the story, the big, black, drooping Stetson. It was not at the proper angle, the proper rakish angle for so young a Navajo. There was no song, and that was not in keeping either. There should have been at least a humming, a faint, all-to-himself "he he he heya," for it was a good horse he was riding, a slender-legged, high-stepping buckskin that would race the wind with light knee-urging. This was a day for singing, a warm winter day, when the touch of the sun upon the back belied the snow high on distant mountains.

Wind warmed by the sun touched his high-boned cheeks like flicker feathers, and still he rode on silently, deeper into Little Canyon, until the red rock walls rose straight upward from the stream bed and only a narrow piece of blue sky hung above. Abruptly the sky widened where the canyon walls were pushed back to make a wide place, as though in ancient times an angry stream had tried to go all ways at once.

This was home—this wide place in the canyon—levels of jagged rock and levels of rich red earth. This was home to Chee, the rider of the buckskin, as it had been to many generations before him.

He stopped his horse at the stream and sat looking across the narrow ribbon of water to the bare-branched peach trees. He was seeing them each springtime with their age-gnarled limbs transfigured beneath veils of blossom pink; he was seeing them in autumn laden with their yellow fruit, small and sweet. Then his eyes searched out the indistinct furrows of the fields beside the stream, where each year the corn and beans and squash drank thirstily of the overflow from summer rains. Chee was trying to outweigh today's bitter betrayal of hope by gathering to himself these reminders of the integrity of the land. Land did not cheat! His mind lingered deliberately on all the days spent here in the sun caring for the young plants, his songs to the earth and to the life springing from it—". . . In the middle of the wide field . . . Yellow Corn Boy . . . He has started both ways . . . ," then the harvest and repayment in full measure. Here was the old feeling of wholeness and of oneness with the sun and earth and growing things.

Chee urged the buckskin toward the family compound where, secure in a recess of overhanging rock, was his mother's dome-shaped hogan, red rock and red adobe like the ground on which it nestled. Not far from the hogan was the half-circle of brush like a dark shadow against the canyon wall—corral for sheep and goats. Farther from the hogan, in full circle, stood the horse corral made of heavy cedar branches sternly interlocked. Chee's long thin lips curved into a smile as he passed his daughter's tiny hogan squatted like a round Pueblo oven beside the corral. He remembered the summer day when together they sat back on their heels and plastered wet adobe all about the circling wall of rock and the woven dome of *piñon*[2] twigs. How his family laughed when the Little One herded the bewildered chickens into her tiny hogan as the first snow fell.

Then the smile faded from Chee's lips and his eyes darkened as he tied his horse to a corral post and turned to the strangely empty compound. "Someone has told them," he thought, "and they are inside weeping." He passed his mother's deserted loom on the south side of the hogan and pulled the rude wooden door toward him, bowing his head, hunching his shoulders to get inside.

His mother sat sideways by the center fire, her feet drawn up under her full skirts. Her hands were busy kneading dough in the chipped white basin. With her head down, her voice was muffled when she said, "The meal will soon be ready, son."

Chee passed his father sitting against the wall, hat over his eyes

[2] *Piñon* (pīn'yōn): a type of pine tree yielding edible, nutlike seeds.

as though asleep. He passed his older sister, who sat turning mutton ribs on a crude wire grill over the coals, noticed tears dropping on her hands. "She cared more for my wife than I realized," he thought.

Then because something must be said sometime, he tossed the black Stetson upon a bulging sack of wool and said, "You have heard, then." He could not shut from his mind how confidently he had set the handsome new hat on his head that very morning, slanting the wide brim over one eye: he was going to see his wife, and today he would ask the doctors about bringing her home; last week she had looked so much better.

His sister nodded but did not speak. His mother sniffled and passed her velveteen sleeve beneath her nose. Chee sat down, leaning against the wall. "I suppose I was a fool for hoping all the time. I should have expected this. Few of our people get well from the coughing sickness. But *she* seemed to be getting better."

His mother was crying aloud now and blowing her nose noisily on her skirt. His father sat up, speaking gently to her.

Chee shifted his position and started a cigarette. His mind turned back to the Little One. At least she was too small to understand what had happened—the Little One who had been born three years before in the sanitarium where his wife was being treated for the coughing sickness, the Little One he had brought home to his mother's hogan to be nursed by his sister whose baby was a few months older. As she grew fat-cheeked and sturdy-legged, she followed him about like a shadow; somehow her baby mind had grasped that of all those at the hogan who cared for her and played with her, he—Chee—belonged most to her. She sat cross-legged at his elbow when he worked silver at the forge; she rode before him in the saddle when he drove the horses to water; often she lay wakeful on her sheep pelts until he stretched out for the night in the darkened hogan and she could snuggle warm against him.

Chee blew smoke slowly, and some of the sadness left his dark eyes as he said, "It is not as bad as it might be. It is not as though we are left with nothing."

Chee's sister arose, sobs catching in her throat, and rushed past him out the doorway. Chee sat upright, a terrible fear possessing him. For a moment his mouth could make no sound. Then: "The Little One! Mother, where is she?"

His mother turned her stricken face to him. "Your wife's people came after her this morning. They heard yesterday of their daughter's death through the trader at Red Sands."

Chee started to protest, but his mother shook her head slowly: "I didn't expect they would want the Little One either. But there is nothing you can do. She is a girl child and belongs to her mother's people; it is custom."

Frowning, Chee got to his feet, grinding his cigarette into the dirt floor. "Custom! When did my wife's parents begin thinking about custom? Why, the hogan where they live doesn't even face the East!" He started toward the door. "Perhaps I can overtake them. Perhaps they don't realize how much we want her here with us. I'll ask them to give my daughter back to me. Surely, they won't refuse."

His mother stopped him gently with her outstretched hand. "You couldn't overtake them now. They were in the trader's car. Eat and rest, and think more about this."

"Have you forgotten how things have always been between you and your wife's people?" his father said.

That night, Chee's thoughts were troubled—half-forgotten incidents became disturbingly vivid—but early the next morning he saddled the buckskin and set out for the settlement of Red Sands. Even though his father-in-law, Old Man Fat, might laugh, Chee knew that he must talk to him. There were some things to which Old Man Fat might listen.

Chee rode the first part of the fifteen miles to Red Sands expectantly. The sight of sandstone buttes[3] near Cottonwood Spring reddening in the morning sun brought a song almost to his lips. He twirled his reins in salute to the small boy herding sheep toward many-colored Butterfly Mountain, watched with pleasure

[3] *Buttes* (byōōts): flat-topped hills rising abruptly above the surrounding area.

the feathers of smoke rising against tree-darkened western mesas from the hogans sheltered there. But as he approached the familiar settlement sprawled in mushroom growth along the highway, he began to feel as though a scene from a bad dream was becoming real.

Several cars were parked around the trading store, which was built like two log hogans side by side, with red gas pumps in front and a sign across the tar-paper roofs: *Red Sands Trading Post—Groceries Gasoline Cold Drinks Sandwiches Indian Curios.* Back of the trading post an unpainted frame house and outbuildings squatted on the drab, treeless land. Chee and the Little One's mother had lived there when they stayed with his wife's people. That was according to custom—living with one's wife's people—but Chee had never been convinced that it was custom alone which prompted Old Man Fat and his wife to insist that their daughter bring her husband to live at the trading post.

Beside the Post was a large hogan of logs, with brightly painted pseudo-Navajo designs on the roof—a hogan with smoke-smudged windows and a garish blue door which faced north to the highway. Old Man Fat had offered Chee a hogan like this one. The trader would build it if he and his wife would live there and Chee would work at his forge making silver jewelry where tourists could watch him. But Chee had asked instead for a piece of land for a cornfield and help in building a hogan far back from the highway and a corral for the sheep he had brought to this marriage.

A cold wind blowing down from the mountains began to whistle about Chee's ears. It flapped the gaudy Navajo rugs which were hung in one long, bright line to attract tourists. It swayed the sign *Navajo Weaver at Work* beside the loom where Old Man Fat's wife sat hunched in her striped blanket, patting the colored thread of a design into place with a wooden comb. Tourists stood watching the weaver. More tourists stood in a knot before the hogan where the sign said: *See Inside a Real Navajo Home 25¢.*

Then the knot seemed to unravel as a few people returned to their cars; some had cameras; and there against the blue door Chee saw the Little One standing uncertainly. The wind was plucking at her new purple blouse and wide green skirt; it freed truant strands of soft dark hair from the meager queue[4] into which it had been tied with white yarn.

"Isn't she cunning!" one of the women tourists was saying as she turned away.

Chee's lips tightened as he began to look around for Old Man Fat. Finally he saw him passing among the tourists collecting coins.

Then the Little One saw Chee. The uncertainty left her face, and she darted through the crowd as her father swung down from his horse. Chee lifted her in his arms, hugging her tight. While he listened to her breathless chatter, he watched Old Man Fat bearing down on them, scowling.

As his father-in-law walked heavily across the graveled lot, Chee was reminded of a statement his mother sometimes made: "When you see a fat Navajo, you see one who hasn't worked for what he has."

Old Man Fat was fattest in the middle. There was indolence in his walk even though he seemed to hurry, indolence in his cheeks so plump they made his eyes squint, eyes now smoldering with anger.

Some of the tourists were getting into their cars and driving away. The old man said belligerently to Chee, "Why do you come here? To spoil our business? To drive people away?"

"I came to talk with you," Chee answered, trying to keep his voice steady as he faced the old man.

"We have nothing to talk about," Old Man Fat blustered and did not offer to touch Chee's extended hand.

"It's about the Little One." Chee settled his daughter more comfortably against his hip as he weighed carefully all the words he had planned to say. "We are going to miss her very much. It wouldn't be so bad if we knew that *part* of each year she could be with us. That might help you too. You and your wife are no longer young people and you have no young ones here to depend upon." Chee chose his next words remembering the thriftlessness of his wife's parents, and their greed. "Perhaps we could share

[4] *Queue* (kyōō): a braid or pigtail.

the care of this little one. Things are good with us. So much snow this year will make lots of grass for the sheep. We have good land for corn and melons."

Chee's words did not have the expected effect. Old Man Fat was enraged. "Farmers, all of you! Long-haired farmers! Do you think everyone must bend his back over the short-handled hoe in order to have food to eat?" His tone changed as he began to brag a little. "We not only have all the things from cans at the trader's, but when the Pueblos come past here on their way to town, we buy their salty jerked mutton, young corn for roasting, dried sweet peaches."

Chee's dark eyes surveyed the land along the highway as the old man continued to brag about being "progressive." *He* no longer was tied to the land. He and his wife made money easily and could *buy* all the things they wanted. Chee realized too late that he had stumbled into the old argument between himself and his wife's parents. They had never understood his feeling about the land—that a man took care of his land and it in turn took care of him. Old Man Fat and his wife scoffed at him, called him a Pueblo farmer, all during that summer when he planted and weeded and harvested. Yet they ate the green corn in their mutton stews, and the chili paste from the fresh ripe chilis, and the tortillas from the corn meal his wife ground. None of this working and sweating in the sun for Old Man Fat, who talked proudly of his easy way of living—collecting money from the trader who rented this strip of land beside the highway, collecting money from the tourists.

Yet Chee had once won that argument. His wife had shared his belief in the integrity of the earth, that jobs and people might fail one, but the earth never would. After that first year she had turned from her own people and gone with Chee to Little Canyon.

Old Man Fat was reaching for the Little One. "Don't be coming here with plans for my daughter's daughter," he warned. "If you try to make trouble, I'll take the case to the government man in town."

The impulse was strong in Chee to turn and ride off while he still had the Little One in his arms. But he knew his time of victory would be short. His own family would uphold the old custom of children, especially girl children, belonging to the mother's people. He would have to give his daughter up if the case were brought before the headman of Little Canyon, and certainly he would have no better chance before a strange white man in town.

He handed the bewildered Little One to her grandfather who stood watching every movement suspiciously. Chee asked, "If I brought you a few things for the Little One, would that be making trouble? Some velvet for a blouse, or some of the jerky she likes so well . . . this summer's melon?"

Old Man Fat backed away from him. "Well," he hesitated, as some of the anger disappeared from his face and beads of greed shone in his eyes. "Well," he repeated. Then as the Little One began to squirm in his arms and cry, he said, "No! No! Stay away from here, you and all your family."

The sense of his failure deepened as Chee rode back to Little Canyon. But it was not until he sat with his family that evening in the hogan, while the familiar bustle of meal preparing went on about him, that he began to doubt the wisdom of the things he'd always believed. He smelled the coffee boiling and the oily fragrance of chili powder dusted into the bubbling pot of stew; he watched his mother turning round crusty fried bread in the small black skillet. All around him was plenty—a half of mutton hanging near the door, bright strings of chilis drying, corn hanging by the braided husks, cloth bags of dried peaches. Yet in his heart was nothing.

He heard the familiar sounds of the sheep outside the hogan, the splash of water as his father filled the long drinking trough from the water barrel. When his father came in, Chee could not bring himself to tell a second time of the day's happenings. He watched his wiry, soft-spoken father while his mother told the story, saw his father's queue of graying hair quiver as he nodded his head with sympathetic exclamations.

Chee's doubting, acrid thoughts kept forming: Was it wisdom his father had passed on to him, or was his inheritance only the stubbornness of a long-haired Navajo resisting change? Take care of the land and it will take care of you. True, the land had always given him food, but now food was not enough. Perhaps if he had gone to school, he would have learned a different kind of wisdom, something to help him now. A schoolboy might even be able to speak convincingly to this government man whom Old Man Fat threatened to call, instead of sitting here like a clod of earth itself—Pueblo farmer indeed. What had the land to give that would restore his daughter?

In the days that followed, Chee herded sheep. He got up in the half-light, drank the hot coffee his mother had ready, then started the flock moving. It was necessary to drive the sheep a long way from the hogan to find good winter forage. Sometimes Chee met friends or relatives who were on their way to town or to the road camp where they hoped to get work; then there was friendly banter and an exchange of news. But most of the days seemed endless; he could not walk far enough or fast enough from his memories of the Little One or from his bitter thoughts. Sometimes it seemed his daughter trudged beside him, so real he could almost hear her footsteps—the muffled pad-pad of little feet clad in deerhide. In the glare of a snowbank he would see her vivid face, brown eyes sparkling. Mingling with the tinkle of sheep bells he heard her laughter.

When, weary of following the small sharp hoof marks that crossed and recrossed in the snow, he sat down in the shelter of a rock, it was only to be reminded that in his thoughts he had forsaken his brotherhood with the earth and sun and growing things. If he remembered times when he had flung himself against the earth to rest, to lie there in the sun until he could no longer feel where he left off and the earth began, it was to remember also that now he sat like an alien against the same earth; the belonging-together was gone. The earth was one thing and he was another.

It was during the days when he herded sheep that Chee decided he must leave Little Canyon. Perhaps he would take a job silversmithing for one of the traders in town. Perhaps, even though he spoke little English, he could get a job at the road camp with his cousins; he would ask them about it.

Springtime transformed the mesas. The peach trees in the canyon were shedding fragrance and pink blossoms on the gentled wind. The sheep no longer foraged for the yellow seeds of chamiso[5] but ranged near the hogan with the long-legged new lambs, eating tender young grass.

Chee was near the hogan on the day his cousins rode up with the message for which he waited. He had been watching with mixed emotions while his father and his sister's husband cleared the fields beside the stream.

"The boss at the camp says he needs an extra hand, but he wants to know if you'll be willing to go with the camp when they move it to the other side of the town?" The tall cousin shifted his weight in the saddle.

The other cousin took up the explanation. "The work near here will last only until the new cutoff beyond Red Sands is finished. After that, the work will be too far away for you to get back here often."

That was what Chee had wanted—to get away from Little Canyon—yet he found himself not so interested in the job beyond town as in this new cutoff which was almost finished. He pulled a blade of grass, split it thoughtfully down the center, as he asked questions of his cousins. Finally he said: "I need to think more about this. If I decide on this job, I'll ride over."

Before his cousins were out of sight down the canyon, Chee was walking toward the fields, a bold plan shaping in his mind. As the plan began to flourish, wild and hardy as young tumbleweed, Chee added his own voice softly to the song his father was singing: ". . . In the middle of the wide field . . . Yellow Corn Boy . . . I wish to put in."

Chee walked slowly around the field, the rich red earth yielding to his footsteps. His plan depended upon this land and upon the things he remembered most about his wife's people.

[5] *Chamiso* (chə·mē'sō): a shrub that forms dense thickets.

Through planting time Chee worked zealously and tirelessly. He spoke little of the large new field he was planting, because he felt so strongly that just now this was something between himself and the land. The first days he was ever stooping, piercing the ground with the pointed stick, placing the corn kernels there, walking around the field and through it, singing, ". . . His track leads into the ground . . . Yellow Corn Boy . . . his track leads into the ground." After that, each day Chee walked through his field watching for the tips of green to break through; first a few spikes in the center and then more and more, until the corn in all parts of the field was above ground. Surely, Chee thought, if he sang the proper songs, if he cared for this land faithfully, it would not forsake him now, even though through the lonely days of winter he had betrayed the goodness of the earth in his thoughts.

Through the summer Chee worked long days, the sun hot upon his back, pulling weeds from around young corn plants; he planted squash and pumpkin; he terraced a small piece of land near his mother's hogan and planted carrots and onions and the moisture-loving chili. He was increasingly restless. Finally he told his family what he hoped the harvest from this land would bring him. Then the whole family waited with him, watching the corn: the slender graceful plants that waved green arms and bent to embrace each other as young winds wandered through the field, the maturing plants flaunting their pollen-laden tassels in the sun, the tall and sturdy parent corn with new-formed ears and a froth of purple, red, and yellow corn-beards against the dusty emerald of broad leaves.

Summer was almost over when Chee slung the bulging packs across two pack ponies. His mother helped him tie the heavy rolled pack behind the saddle of the buckskin. Chee knotted the new yellow kerchief about his neck a little tighter, gave the broad black hat brim an extra tug, but these were only gestures of assurance and he knew it. The land had not failed him. That part was done. But this he was riding into? Who could tell?

When Chee arrived at Red Sands, it was as he had expected to find it—no cars on the highway. His cousins had told him that even the Pueblo farmers were using the new cutoff to town. The barren gravel around the Red Sands Trading Post was deserted. A sign banged against the dismantled gas pumps: *Closed until further notice.*

Old Man Fat came from the crude summer shelter built beside the log hogan from a few branches of scrub cedar and the sides of wooden crates. He seemed almost friendly when he saw Chee.

"Get down, my son," he said, eyeing the bulging packs. There was no bluster in his voice today, and his face sagged, looking somewhat saddened, perhaps because his cheeks were no longer quite full enough to push his eyes upward at the corners. "You are going on a journey?"

Chee shook his head. "Our fields gave us so much this year, I thought to sell or trade this to the trader. I didn't know he was no longer here."

Old Man Fat sighed, his voice dropping to an injured tone. "He says he and his wife are going to rest this winter; then after that he'll build a place up on the new highway."

Chee moved as though to be traveling on, then jerked his head toward the pack ponies. "Anything you need?"

"I'll ask my wife," Old Man Fat said as he led the way to the shelter. "Maybe she has a little money. Things have not been too good with us since the trader closed. Only a few tourists come this way." He shrugged his shoulders. "And with the trader gone —no credit."

Chee was not deceived by his father-in-law's unexpected confidences. He recognized them as a hopeful bid for sympathy and, if possible, something for nothing. Chee made no answer. He was thinking that so far he had been right about his wife's parents: their thriftlessness had left them with no resources to last until Old Man Fat found another easy way of making a living.

Old Man Fat's wife was in the shelter working at her loom. She turned rather wearily when her husband asked with noticeable deference if she would give him money to buy supplies. Chee surmised that the only income here was from his mother-in-law's weaving.

She peered around the corner of the shelter at the laden ponies, and then she looked at Chee. "What do you have there, my son?"

Chee smiled to himself as he turned to pull the pack from one of the ponies, dragged it to the shelter where he untied the ropes. Pumpkins and hard-shelled squash tumbled out, and the ears of corn—pale yellow husks fitting firmly over plump ripe kernels, blue corn, red corn, yellow corn, many-colored corn, ears and ears of it—tumbled into every corner of the shelter.

"Yooooh," Old Man Fat's wife exclaimed as she took some of the ears in her hands. Then she glanced up at her son-in-law. "But we have no money for all this. We have sold almost everything we own—even the brass bed that stood in the hogan."

Old Man Fat's brass bed. Chee concealed his amusement as he started back for another pack. That must have been a hard parting. Then he stopped for, coming from the cool darkness of the hogan was the Little One, rubbing her eyes as though she had been asleep. She stood for a moment in the doorway, and Chee saw that she was dirty, barefoot, her hair uncombed, her little blouse shorn of all its silver buttons. Then she ran toward Chee, her arms outstretched. Heedless of Old Man Fat and his wife, her father caught her in his arms, her hair falling in a dark cloud across his face, the sweetness of her laughter warm against his shoulder.

It was the haste within him to get this slow waiting game played through to the finish that made Chee speak unwisely. It was the desire to swing her before him in the saddle and ride fast to Little Canyon that prompted his words. "The money doesn't matter. You still have something. . . ."

Chee knew immediately that he had overspoken. The old woman looked from him to the corn spread before her. Unfriendliness began to harden in his father-in-law's face. All the old arguments between himself and his wife's people came pushing and crowding in between them now.

Old Man Fat began kicking the ears of corn back onto the canvas as he eyed Chee angrily. "And you rode all the way over here thinking that for a little food we would give up our daughter's daughter?"

Chee did not wait for the old man to reach for the Little One. He walked dazedly to the shelter, rubbing his cheek against her soft dark hair, and put her gently into her grandmother's lap. Then he turned back to the horses. He had failed. By his own haste he had failed. He swung into the saddle, his hand touching the roll behind it. Should he ride on into town?

Then he dismounted, scarcely glancing at Old Man Fat, who stood uncertainly at the corner of the shelter, listening to his wife. "Give me a hand with this other pack of corn, grandfather," Chee said, carefully keeping the small bit of hope from his voice.

Puzzled, but willing, Old Man Fat helped carry the other pack to the shelter, opening it to find more corn as well as carrots and round, pale yellow onions. Chee went back for the roll behind the buckskin's saddle and carried it to the entrance of the shelter, where he cut the ropes and gave the canvas a nudge with his toe. Tins of coffee rolled out, small plump cloth bags; jerked meat from several butcherings spilled from a flour sack; and bright red chilis splashed like flames against the dust.

"I will leave all this anyhow," Chee told them. "I would not want my daughter nor even you old people to go hungry."

Old Man Fat picked up a shiny tin of coffee, then put it down. With trembling hands he began to untie one of the cloth bags—dried sweet peaches.

The Little One had wriggled from her grandmother's lap, unheeded, and was on her knees, digging her hands into the jerked meat.

"There is almost enough food here to last all winter," Old Man Fat's wife sought the eyes of her husband.

Chee said, "I meant it to be enough. But that was when I thought you might send the Little One back with me." He looked down at his daughter noisily sucking jerky. Her mouth, both fists, were full of it. "I am sorry that you feel you cannot bear to part with her."

Old Man Fat's wife brushed a straggly wisp of gray hair from her forehead as she turned to look at the Little One. Old Man Fat was looking too. And it was not a thing to see. For in that moment the Little One ceased to be their daughter's daughter and became just another mouth to feed.

"And why not?" the old woman asked wearily.

Chee was settled in the saddle, the barefooted Little One before him. He urged the buckskin faster, and his daughter clutched his shirtfront. The purpling mesas flung back the echo: ". . . My corn embrace each other. In the middle of the wide field . . . Yellow Corn Boy embrace each other."

I HAVE BOWED BEFORE THE SUN

ANNA LEE WALTERS PAWNEE-OTOE

This poetic vision by an Oklahoma poet and painter is reminiscent of the purification rites her people once underwent.

My name is "I am living."
My home is all directions and is everlasting.
Instructed and carried to you by the wind,
I have felt the feathers in pale clouds and bowed before the Sun
who watches me from a blanket of faded blue.
In a gentle whirlwind I was shaken,
made to see on earth in many ways.
And when in awe my mouth fell open,
I tasted a fine red clay.
Its flavor has remained after uncounted days.
This gave me cause to drink from a crystal stream
that only I have seen.
So I listened to all its flowing wisdom
and learned from it a Song—
This song the wind and I
have since sung together.
Unknowing, I was encircled by its water and cleansed.
Naked and damp, I was embraced and dried
by the warmth of your presence.
Dressed forever in the scent of dry cedar,

Eskimo mother and child. Photograph by Tessa MacIntosh.

I am purified and free.
And I will not allow you to ignore me.
I have brought to you a gift.
It is all I have but it is yours.
You may reach out and enfold it.
It is only the strength in the caress of a gentle breeze,
But it will carry you to meet the eagle in the sky.
My name is "I am living." I am here.
My name is "I am living." I am here.

WE LIVE WITH THE LAND

JEANNIE ALIKA ATYA ESKIMO

Ms. Atya is a resident of Broughton Island, which is north of the Arctic Circle in the Canadian Northwest Territories.

I am going to speak for Eskimos as an Eskimo. Most white people know of us only from books which tell about igloos and the giant steps forward the Eskimos are supposed to be taking.

The difference between the Eskimo and the white man is the color of the skin, the language, culture, values, and outlook on life. The white man has a strong culture which he forces on us Eskimo. The white man has his concept of life. His meals are set on time. His years are dictated by time—time to go to school, college, work, promotion, and retirement.

We Eskimos eat when we are hungry. The hunter hunts whenever and wherever the hunting is good. We live with the land instead of against it.

The white man came and forced missionaries, diseases, and, today, confusion on the Eskimo. White man teaches his ways—he's going too fast. He makes decisions for us but pretends that we are making them. He takes away our children, our land, our language, our culture, and our pride.

White people must protest what the government is doing. If they don't protest, they'll be guilty of destroying us. Then they will write books about it and say, "What a pity!" But it will be too late.

I DREAM LONG-NECK WOMAN

I feel the child cry
from in my womb.
Hold him on my back, I dream
warm in beads and leather
Rock him
swinging
on a pine
straight, the poles of my lodge
red stars on the summer sky.

Then he comes
and goes
walking concrete
touching steel
Oh!
to hold him in until
the earth is whole again.

Embarking–Kutenai. Edward S. Curtis, 1910.

SOURCES AND CREDITS

p. vii Untitled . . . Walter Lowenfels, ed., *From the Belly of the Shark* (New York: Vintage Books, 1973), p. 57, by permission of the estate of Walter Lowenfels, Manna Lowenfels-Perpelitt, literary executor.

Part I

Section 1

p. 7 Grandmother's Prayer . . . Ruth Bunzel, *Zuñi Ritual Poetry,* 47th Annual Report, Bureau of American Ethnology (Washington, D.C.: Smithsonian Institution, 1932), p. 635.

p. 9 For Me and My First . . . Florence Shipek, *Autobiography of Delfina Cuero,* as told to Florence Shipek, Mrs. Rosalie Pinto Robertson, interpreter (Los Angeles: Dawson's Book Shop, 1968), pp. 44–46, by permission, Mrs. Shipek and Dawson's Book Shop. Reprinted by Malki Museum, Morongo Indian Reservation, Banning, California.

p. 10 Lullaby . . . Herbert J. Spinden, *Songs of the Tewa* (New York: Exposition of Indian Tribal Arts, Inc., 1933), p. 81. Reprinted by AMS Press, New York, 1976.

p. 11 The Father . . . Sarah Winnemucca Hopkins, *Life Among the Piutes* (Bishop, Calif.: Chalfant Press, 1883), pp. 49–50. Reprinted by Sierra Media, Inc., Bishop, California, 1969.

p. 13 There Was Love . . . Louise Udall, *Me and Mine: The Life Story of Helen Sekaquaptewa,* as told to Louise Udall (Tucson: University of Arizona Press, 1969), pp. 6–7, by permission.

p. 14 My People Teach . . . Sarah Winnemucca Hopkins, *Life Among the Piutes,* pp. 45, 51.

p. 15 Woman's Song . . . Alice Fletcher, *The Hako: A Pawnee Ceremony,* 22nd Annual Report, Bureau of American Ethnology (Washington, D.C.: Smithsonian Institution, 1904), pp. 13–372.

p. 15 Dorothy Eber, ed., *Pitseolak: Pictures Out of My Life* (Seattle: University of Washington Press by arrangement with Design Collaborative Books, Montreal, 1972), pp. 1–6, by permission.

Section 2

p. 17 Corn-Grinding . . . Natalie Curtis, *The Indians' Book* (New York: Harper and Brothers, 1907), p. 430.

p. 19 There Is a . . . Underhill, *Autobiography of a Papago Woman,* pp. 5–11, 22–23.

p. 24 A Happy . . . Gilbert Wilson, *Waheenee: An Indian Girl's Story,* as told to Gilbert Wilson (Minneapolis, Minn.: Webb Publishing Co., 1921), pp. 16–17, 117–118, by permission.

p. 26 Being a Young Woman . . . Truman Michelson, *The Autobiography of a Fox Indian Woman,* 40th Annual Report, Bureau of American Ethnology (Washington, D.C.: Smithsonian Institution, 1925), pp. 303–307.

p. 27 We Were Never . . . Nancy Oestreich Lurie, *Mountain Wolf Woman* (Ann Arbor: University of Michigan Press, 1961), pp. 87–88, by permission.

p. 30 The Children . . . Udall, *Me and Mine,* pp. 91–93, 104–105, 124–125.

Section 3

p. 32 Young Woman's Song . . . Frances Densmore, *Chippewa Music II,* Bureau of American Ethnology Bulletin No. 53 (Washington, D.C.: Smithsonian Institution, 1913), p. 300.

p. 32 And So I . . . Wilson, *Waheenee,* pp. 117–126.

p. 37 I Cried . . . Lurie, *Mountain Wolf Woman,* pp. 29–30.

Section 4

p. 39 I'm a Little Woman . . . Tom Lowenstein, trans., *Eskimo Poems from Canada and Greenland* by Knud Rasmussen (Pittsburgh, Pa.: University of Pittsburgh Press, 1973), p. 34, by permission.

p. 40 When I Married . . . Shipek, *Autobiography of Delfina Cuero,* pp. 55–57.

p. 42 The Women Know . . . Hopkins, *Life Among the Piutes,* pp. 52–53.

p. 44 Song of the Rejected . . . Lowenstein, trans., *Eskimo Poems from Canada and Greenland,* pp. 35–36.

p. 45 I Said I Am Going . . . Underhill, *Autobiography of a Papago Woman,* pp. 53–55.

p. 48 Songs of Divorce . . . Frances Densmore, *Music of the Indians of British Columbia,* Bureau of American Ethnology Bulletin No. 136 (Washington, D.C.: Smithsonian Institution, 1943), pp. 84–85.

Section 5

p. 49 Love-Charm Song . . . Densmore, *Chippewa Music,* Bureau of American Ethnology Bulletin No. 45 (Washington, D.C.: Smithsonian Institution, 1910), p. 90.

p. 50 The Peoples Who . . . Joseph Epes Brown, ed. and recorder, *The Sacred Pipe: Black Elk's Account of the Seven Rites of the Oglala Sioux* (Norman: University of Oklahoma Press, 1953), p. 7, copyright 1953 by University of Oklahoma Press, by permission.

p. 50 Ruth Bunzel, *Introduction to Zuñi Ceremonialism,* 47th Annual Report, Bureau of American Ethnology, pp. 483–484.

p. 52 Help Peoples . . . David E. Jones, *Sanapia: Comanche Medicine Woman* (New York: Holt, Rinehart & Winston, 1972), p. 31, by permission.

p. 53 I Got the Power . . . *Ibid.,* pp. 44–45.

p. 54 Dream Song . . . Densmore, *Papago Music,* Bureau of American Ethnology Bulletin No. 90 (Washington, D.C.: Smithsonian Institution, 1929), p. 206.

p. 55 I Move . . . Lurie, *Mountain Wolf Woman,* p. 91.

p. 57 A Woman Shaman's . . . Lowenstein, trans., *Eskimo Poems from Canada and Greenland,* p. 27.

Section 6

p. 58 In the Spirit-Land . . . Hopkins, *Life Among the Piutes,* pp. 54–55.

p. 59 Owl Woman's . . . Densmore, *Papago Music,* p. 126.

p. 59 Prayer of a Mother . . . Franz Boas, *Religion of the Kwakiutl Indians,* Contributions to Anthropology, vol. 10 (New York: Columbia University Press, 1930), p. 202, by permission.

p. 60 The Widow's Song . . . Lowenstein, trans., *Eskimo Poems from Canada and Greenland,* pp. 19–20.

p. 62 They Would Not . . . Ruth Bunzel, *Zuñi Texts, American Ethnological Society,* vol. 15 (New York: G. E. Stechert Co., 1933), pp. 93–96, by permission of American Ethnological Society.

p. 64 A Woman's Song . . . From John R. Swanton, *Tlingit Myths and Texts,* Bureau of American Ethnology Bulletin No. 39 (Washington, D.C.: Smithsonian Institution, 1909), pp. 410–411.

Section 7

p. 65 My Poor . . . Hopkins, *Life Among the Piutes,* pp. 209–213.

p. 66 We Do Not Want . . . Louis Thomas Jones, *Aboriginal American Oratory* (Los Angeles, Calif.: Southwest Museum, 1965), p. 115, by permission.

p. 68 Eber, *Pitseolak: Pictures Out of My Life,* pp. 40–47, 68–76.

p. 69 I Cannot Forget . . . Wilson, *Waheenee,* pp. 175–176.

p. 70 The White People . . . Dorothy Lee, Freedom and Culture, "An-

thropology," in Hoxie N. Fairchild, *et al., Religious Perspectives in College Teaching* (New York: The Ronald Press, 1952), p. 340, copyright 1952, by permission.
p. 71 My Way Is . . . Jones, *Sanapia*, p. 46.

Part II

Section 1
p. 80 I See Strange . . . Program book of American Indian Festival (Chicago: Field Museum and American Indian Center, September–October 1968), by permission.
p. 81 The Twentieth-Century . . . Laura Wittstock to Jane Katz (interviewer), December 1975, by permission of Laura Wittstock.
p. 83 In the Shallows . . . *Akwesasne Notes* (Mohawk Nation, Rooseveltown, N.Y.), Early Summer 1975, by permission.
p. 84 August 24 . . . *South Dakota Review*, Summer 1969, p. 106, by permission of Donna Whitewing and John Milton, eds.
p. 84 My Grandmother . . . Earl Shorris, *Death of the Great Spirit* (New York: Simon & Schuster, 1971), pp. 191–197, by permission.
p. 88 A Holding Battle . . . *Wassaja*, January 1976. Copyright © 1976 by American Indian Historical Society, by permission.
p. 89 I Don't Like . . . Eskimo woman to Nancy McNeil (interviewer), from "Arctic High Rise," *Akwesasne Notes* tape library, by permission of Louis T. Cook.
p. 90 We Will Survive . . . Shorris, *Death of the Great Spirit*, p. 144.

Section 2
p. 91 On the Reservation . . . *Time of the Indian* (St. Paul, Minn.: Community Programs in the Arts & Sciences [COMPAS], 1975), by permission of Molly La Berge, Director.
p. 93 We Lived on . . . Louise Hiett to Steve Plummer (interviewer), June 1971, Oral History Center, Institute of American Indian Studies, University of South Dakota, by permission of Joseph Cash, Director.
p. 94 I Always Felt . . . Gertrude Buckanaga to Jane Katz (interviewer), January 1976, by permission of Gertrude Buckanaga.
p. 95 News from Old Crow . . . Kent Gooderham, ed., *I Am an Indian* (Toronto, Canada: J. M. Dent & Sons Limited, 1969), pp. 119–122, by permission of Clarke, Irwin and Company Limited.
p. 99 Return to the Home . . . *Akwesasne Notes*, November–December 1970, by permission.
p. 103 There Is No . . . From *Helping a People to Understand*, pamphlet of the Nursing Advisory Service, National Tuberculosis Association (now the American Lung Association). Quoted in Edgar Cahn and David W.

Hearne, eds., *Our Brother's Keeper: The Indian in White America* (New York: New American Library, 1975), pp. 65–66.
p. 104 I Want to Be a Christian . . . Laura Ziegler to Gerald Wolff (interviewer), August 1971, Oral History Center, by permission.
p. 105 Wool Season . . . *American Poetry Review,* September–October 1975. Copyright © 1975 by Paula Gunn Allen, by permission of Paula Gunn Allen and *American Poetry Review.*
p. 106 Our Children Know . . . Lila McCortney to Blix Ruskay (interviewer), December 1975, by permission of Blix Ruskay.

Section 3
p. 109 If the Children . . . Lila McCortney to Blix Ruskay.
p. 110 Ol' Uncle Sam . . . Joseph Cash and Herbert Hoover, eds., *To Be an Indian* (New York: Holt, Rinehart & Winston, 1971), pp. 86–88, by permission.
p. 111 I Am a Metis . . . Yvonne Monkman to B. A. Hershfeld (interviewer), January 1976, by permission of B. A. Hershfeld.
p. 112 Everybody Always . . . Winifred Jourdain to Jane Katz (interviewer), February 1976, by permission of Winifred Jourdain.
p. 114 If I Had a Chance . . . Louise Hiett to Steve Plummer.
p. 114 Ah, I Knew Everybody . . . Sylvia Whipple to Herbert Hoover (interviewer), May 1972, Oral History Center, by permission.
p. 115 Feel the Coming . . . by permission of Melanie Ellis.
p. 116 Education . . . Laura Wittstock to Jane Katz.
p. 116 Who Was Really . . . Rose Mary Barstow to Jane Katz (interviewer), March 1976.
p. 119 I Wish I Could . . . *Time of the Indian.*

Section 4
p. 120 Parents Are . . . Terry Morris, "A Woman Who Gives a Damn," *Redbook,* February 1970. Copyright © 1970, by permission of Redbook Publishing Co.
p. 122 Indian Women . . . Gertrude Buckanaga to Jane Katz.
p. 122 I Am a Lakota . . . Bea Medicine, "Role and Function of Indian Women," *Indian Education* (National Indian Education Association [NIEA]), January 1977, pp. 4–5, by permission of Bea Medicine and NIEA.
p. 123 Indian Medicine . . . Harley Sorenson, *Minneapolis Tribune,* September 2, 1973, excerpted by permission.
p. 125 Beating the . . . Susan Berman, *Courier-Post* (Camden, N.J.), February 4, 1971, excerpted by permission.
p. 126 The Woman Is . . . Maggie Wilson, *Arizona Republic,* September 24, 1972, excerpted by permission.
p. 127 Love, Grandma . . . *Akwesasne Notes,* Summer 1975, by permission.

Section 5
p. 129 It's Almost . . . Lila McCortney to Blix Ruskay.
p. 130 I Have a House . . . Laura Ziegler to Gerald Wolff.
p. 130 The Obstacles . . . Winifred Jourdain to Jane Katz.
p. 131 Can I Say . . . *Akwesasne Notes,* Spring 1972, by permission.
p. 133 Don't See No . . . *Voices from Wounded Knee, 1973: The People Are Standing Up* (Mohawk Nation, Rooseveltown, N.Y.: *Akwesasne Notes,* 1974), pp. 236–237, by permission.
p. 136 On My Reservation . . . *Navajo Times* (The Navajo Nation, Window Rock, Ariz.), December 14, 1972, by permission.
p. 137 We Learned . . . *Voices from Wounded Knee, 1973,* pp. 181–183.
p. 139 There Were No . . . *Akwesasne Notes,* Autumn 1974, by permission.
p. 141 White-Indian . . . *The Indian Historian,* Spring 1975, p. 49. Copyright © 1975, by permission of American Indian Historical Society and Jeannette Henry, editor.
p. 142 The Brave-Hearted . . . *Akwesasne Notes,* Early Summer 1976, by permission.
p. 144 Gasification . . . Excerpts from a document submitted March 1975 by Claudeen Bates Arthur to the United States Bureau of Reclamation, by permission of Claudeen Bates Arthur.
p. 145 A Huge Gas . . . *Akwesasne Notes,* Early Winter 1975, by permission.
p. 146 We're Talking . . . Ramona Bennett interview, November 1970, from *Akwesasne Notes* tape library, by permission of *Akwesasne Notes.*
p. 148 The Power . . . "The Roles and Rights of Native Indian Women," address by Ada Deer to North American Indian Women's Association (NAIWA), Northern Michigan University, June 12, 1975, by permission of Ada Deer and Robert R. Bailey, Director, American Indian Programs, N.M.U., Marquette, Michigan.

Section 6
p. 152 Once Again . . . *South Dakota Review,* Summer 1969, by permission of Liz Sohappy and John Milton, ed.
p. 153 To Preserve . . . Stan Steiner, *The New Indians* (New York: Harper & Row, 1968), pp. 288–289, by permission.
p. 154 Diné . . . *South Dakota Review,* Winter 1974/75, by permission of Paula Gunn Allen and John Milton, ed.
p. 156 The Man to Send . . . Kenneth Rosen, ed., *The Man to Send Rain Clouds* (New York: The Viking Press, 1974). Copyright © 1969 by Leslie Chapman, by permission of The Viking Press.
p. 162 I Know Who . . . Margaret Vickers to Jane Katz (interviewer), August 1976, by permission of Margaret Vickers.
p. 163 After He Died . . . Dorothy Eber, ed., *Pitseolak: Pictures Out of My Life* (Seattle: University of Washington Press by arrangement with

Design Collaborative Books [Montreal], 1972), pp. 1, 78, 80. Quatsia Ottochie, interpreter, retranslated by Ann Hanson.

p. 164 Walk in Beauty . . . Maggie Wilson, *Arizona Republic,* November 22, 1974, adapted by permission.

p. 165 Where Mountainlion . . . Leslie Silko, *Laguna Woman* (Greenfield Center, N.Y.: The Greenfield Review Press, 1974). Copyright © 1974 by Leslie Silko, by permission of Leslie Silko.

Section 7

p. 167 How I Came . . . By permission of Wendy Rose.

p. 168 Refuse to Be . . . *Akwesasne Notes,* Early Winter 1976, p. 29, by permission.

p. 172 My People Are the Poor . . . Lowenfels, ed., *From the Belly of the Shark.*

p. 173 We Choose . . . *Akwesasne Notes,* Spring 1975, p. 3, by permission.

p. 176 Chee's Daughter . . . *Common Ground,* Winter 1948, by permission of American Council for Nationalities Service.

p. 190 I Have Bowed . . . Rosen, ed., *The Man to Send Rain Clouds,* p. 177.

p. 192 We Live . . . Jeannie Alika Atya to Nancy McNeil, "Arctic High Rise," from *Akwesasne Notes* tape library, by permission of *Akwesasne Notes.*

p. 193 I Dream . . . *Akwesasne Notes,* Early Summer 1975, by permission.